LITTLE, BROWN
CO
LARGE
PRINT

IN THE BLOOD

APRIL HENRY

Christy Ottaviano Books

LITTLE, BROWN AND COMPANY

LARGE PRINT

Copyright © 2026 by April Henry

All cover and interior images copyright © various contributors at Shutterstock.com

Cover art by Neil Swaab. Cover design by Gabrielle Chang. Cover copyright © 2026 by Hachette Book Group, Inc. Interior design by Michelle Gengaro-Kokmen.

Christy Ottaviano Books
Hachette Book Group
1290 Avenue of the Americas, New York, NY 10104
ChristyOttavianoBooks.com

First Edition: May 2026

Christy Ottaviano Books is an imprint of Little, Brown and Company. The Christy Ottaviano Books name and logo are registered trademarks of Hachette Book Group, Inc.

The publisher is not responsible for websites (or their content) that are not owned by the publisher.

Little, Brown and Company books may be purchased in bulk for business, educational, or promotional use. For information, please contact your local bookseller or the Hachette Book Group Special Markets Department at special.markets@hbgusa.com.

Library of Congress Cataloging-in-Publication Data
Names: Henry, April author
Title: In the blood / April Henry.
Description: First edition. | New York : Little, Brown and Company, 2026. | "Christy Ottaviano Books." | Audience: Ages 12 & up | Summary: When high school senior Tess turns eighteen, she takes a DNA test in hopes of finding her biological parents, but instead discovers links to a religious cult and the elusive Portland Phantom, a serial killer responsible for the deaths of seven young women.
Identifiers: LCCN 2025042315 | ISBN 9780316586214 hardcover | ISBN 9780316586238 ebook
Subjects: CYAC: Family life—Fiction | Identity—Fiction | Parents—Fiction | Serial murderers—Fiction | LCGFT: Novels | Thrillers (Fiction)
Classification: LCC PZ7.H39356 In 2026
LC record available at https://lccn.loc.gov/2025042315

ISBNs: 978-0-316-58621-4 (hardcover), 978-0-316-58623-8 (ebook), 978-0-316-61075-9 (large print)

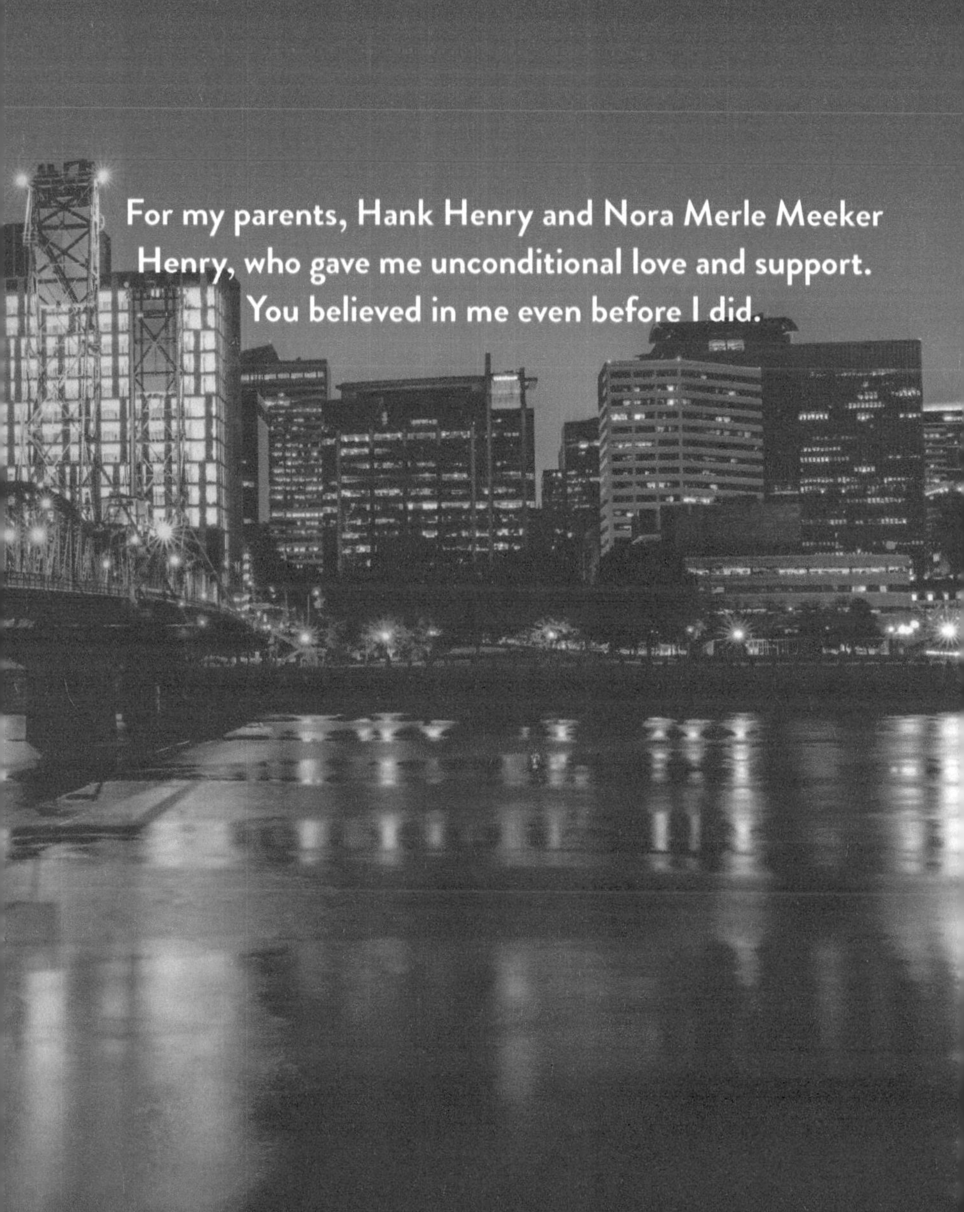

For my parents, Hank Henry and Nora Merle Meeker
Henry, who gave me unconditional love and support.
You believed in me even before I did.

From the Lifetime documentary
Chasing Shadows: The Hunt for the Portland Phantom

On-screen, a quick montage of iconic Portland photos: Pioneer Courthouse Square, a drone view of the city's bridges, a purple-haired barista making a latte, the city's skyline set off by snow-capped Mount Hood, and the marquee for Powell's City of Books.

The appealing images are undercut by an ominous, discordant soundtrack. The montage ends with a large map of the city filling the screen. Photos of a half dozen young women are pinned to it, connected with a web of red string.

As the camera pans from the face of one woman to another, a man's gravelly voice says, "A dark secret lurks in the quiet corners of Portland, Oregon. Once known for its serene landscapes and hipster havens, the city is now haunted by the Portland Phantom, who has murdered seven young women over the last fourteen years."

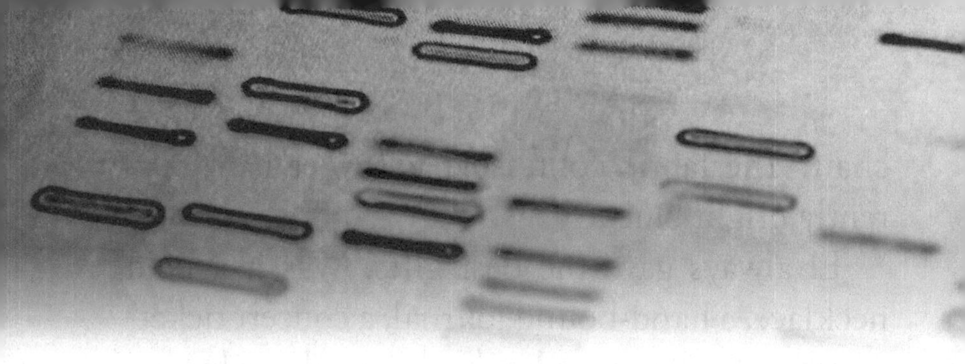

TESSA

Finally

"HAPPY BIRTHDAY!" EL SANG OUT, BOUNDING INTO Tessa's room.

Tessa felt a fizz of excitement as El handed her a book-size package wrapped in floral paper. Tessa wasn't much of a floral person, but she was definitely a present person.

"My birthday's not until next week." As was the start of their senior year. Tessa was always the first in her grade to turn a year older. Despite her words, she was already sliding her finger under the tape.

"I wanted to give it to you in private."

Tessa was sitting on the edge of her bed, and now El flopped down into the bright orange chair. The fabric contrasted with her hair, currently bright blue.

El always gave the best gifts. Was it a bold necklace, a hand-bound journal, a concert ticket? Maybe it really was a book, a new release by one of Tessa's favorite authors.

But she couldn't think of anything El would wait to give her in private.

The wrapping paper finally yielded its secret. A white box printed with an abstract design of leaves. "What's this?" Tessa looked at El. But she already knew.

"It's an Ancestry DNA test." El took a deep breath. "Once you're eighteen, you can finally find out who your real family is."

So that's why El had waited until they were alone. Their friendship had started in third grade, just before Thanksgiving, when their substitute teacher told them their homework would be to create a family tree. The photocopied chart she handed out started with a blank line labeled *Me* and then branched back into lines for *Mother* and *Father*. Past them were lines for four grandparents and then eight great-grandparents.

Thanksgiving, she explained, would be the perfect time to find out more about their family history.

But the only line Tessa could fill out was the first one, for her own name. Tessa Lundgren. The name she'd been given when she was adopted.

The rest of Tessa's family, with their blond hair, blue eyes, and skin that tanned golden brown in the summer, definitely looked like Lundgrens. But Tessa? Her dark hair and eyes and milk-pale skin did not look one bit Scandinavian.

Back then, El hadn't known why Tessa had started to cry, just that she had. El slipped out of her chair and wrapped one arm around Tessa. As El informed the teacher the assignment was "stupid," Tessa balled up the paper and threw it onto the floor.

They both got sent to the principal.

Later, Tessa's normally cheerful mom explained to the substitute how insensitive the assignment was to kids who were adopted, in foster care, or otherwise being raised by people who weren't their biological parents. Afterward, she reiterated to Tessa, "You're special because you were chosen by us. It doesn't matter whether you're biologically ours. You're still our daughter."

At recess the next morning, Tessa told El the truths she normally hid. No one knew who her parents were. As a newborn, she had been left at a fire station without even a note.

But El didn't see it as Tessa being unwanted or discarded. To El, Tessa's past was a mystery with an answer that was probably way cooler than El's regular, boring family.

After that, they spent hours speculating about who Tessa's "real" parents were. As little kids, they were certain her parents were royalty, or at least fabulously wealthy. As they got older, their fantasies expanded. Her parents might be artists, painting masterpieces and living in a cabin in the wilderness. Or elite executives flying on private jets from one high-stakes negotiation to the next. Maybe they were world-renowned scientists making groundbreaking discoveries. In each story, her parents had given her up only because they were too young, too important, or some combination of both.

Now, Tessa stared unseeing at the white box, her mind racing with a thousand doubts and fears. Did she really want to know who her biological family was? Would they even want to know her? Would learning about them change how she felt about herself? Would it change how the only parents she'd ever known saw her?

El's voice pulled Tessa out of her spiral. "You don't have to do it if you don't want to. But think about it. If you don't, you'll never know."

Tessa nodded, but she was remembering the story of Pandora.

When Pandora opened that forbidden box, she unleashed illness and death into the world.

Once Tessa took the test, she couldn't undo it.

TESSA

Instructions

MOST TEACHERS TOOK IT EASY THE FIRST DAY OF school. Not Mr. Prenty, a tall, thin man who reminded Tessa of a long-legged bird. As soon as the bell rang, he clapped his hands.

"Welcome to Bio Two."

Tessa smothered a yawn. It was after lunch, and the room was hot and stuffy.

Two girls in the back row were whispering. Mr. Prenty fell silent, face impassive, until they stopped.

"We have a lot to do this afternoon. Today we'll be partnering up, watching a safety video, and performing a short experiment."

Partnering? Tessa scanned the room for a familiar face.

Mr. Prenty had other plans. "I'll be assigning partners based on last names. And before anyone asks—no, you cannot change partners. In real life, you're going to have to get along with coworkers you have nothing in common with. And in this class, as in life, your success depends on teamwork." He picked up a printout. "Abbott and Andrews. Bancroft and Cooper. Corning and…"

Lundgren was pretty close to the *M*'s. Maybe Tessa would get Bree Madigan? Like her, Bree spent a lot of time in the library.

"Lopez and Lundgren."

So much for getting someone she knew. Tessa couldn't even remember Lopez's first name. Vincent? Victor? She studied his profile out of the corner of her eye. His dark wavy bangs were on the long side, but the rest of his hair was short enough to reveal the curve of one sideburn and a silver hoop earring. He wore a short-sleeved plaid shirt and jeans. As if sensing her gaze, he turned. His dark eyes met hers, his face impassive.

Tessa looked away. Her cheeks felt hot. With her paper-white skin, it was too much to hope the flush didn't show.

"In this class, we'll be working with chemicals,

some of which are hazardous," Mr. Prenty said. "This video will address safety issues."

He dimmed the lights. In the video, actors portraying high school students while appearing to be in their mid-thirties demonstrated how to use exhaust hoods, fire extinguishers, and emergency eyewash stations.

Maybe this class wasn't going to be as boring as Tessa had thought.

Mr. Prenty flipped the lights back on. "We'll be spending the rest of class extracting DNA from strawberries."

DNA. Tessa pictured the Ancestry DNA kit, now hidden in the back of her sweater drawer. She straightened up.

"DNA is an instruction manual for making a living organism. It basically tells it how to develop and function. We'll be using household chemicals to extract DNA from strawberries. A single strand of DNA is too tiny to see with the naked eye. But strawberries have a lot of DNA, and we're going to clump it together so it's visible. Most species have two copies of the genome, one from each parent. But the strawberry actually has eight, contributed by eight parental species."

"It's like a ménage à trois, only it's a ménage à huit!" Trey Cooper joked. He was always joking, but at least this was a smart joke.

Mr. Prenty acted as if he hadn't heard. "You and your partner should pick a lab table and then one person will get supplies. Together, you'll need four strawberries, two plastic cups, a coffee filter, a plastic spoon, a coffee stirrer, and a resealable plastic bag." As he spoke, he wrote each item on the board. "Let's get started."

Tessa and her new lab partner looked at each other across the room. He pointed to an empty black lab table in the middle and she met him there.

"I'm Tessa."

"Victor." He gave her a half smile. The side of his throat was marked with a small black mole, right above two silver chains. Tessa had the irrational urge to put her fingertip on it.

Instead, she said, "I'll get the supplies."

As she did, Mr. Prenty said, "One partner will remove the stems and then put the strawberries inside the plastic bag, seal it, and gently smash them. This lets the solution reach more area."

A few seconds later, Trey pounded his big fist

onto the side of his open bag. Strawberry bits splattered halfway across the room. His partner squealed.

Mr. Prenty frowned. "Mr. Cooper, another such incident and you will be out of this class. Do you understand me?"

Looking chastened, Trey nodded.

"The cells are like water balloons. We'll use detergent to make them pop open, or lyse, releasing the DNA. The other partner should measure two teaspoons of salt and one of detergent into a cup. Then add a half cup of water."

Tessa waited her turn for one of the half dozen measuring cups while Victor lightly thumped his fist on the strawberry bits.

"Swirl the salt and detergent water *gently*." Mr. Prenty emphasized the last word. "That's our extraction liquid. Then have your partner open the plastic bag and pour it in."

Worried about spilling, Tessa rested her fingers on Victor's hand as she tipped the water into the bag. She was hyperconscious of his cool skin.

"Seal it up and work it gently, like you're making a smoothie by hand. The detergent will break open the strawberry cells. The DNA is now collecting in the liquid, but so is a lot of other stuff. Scientifically, it's known as cellular debris, but it's just strawberry schmutz."

Following Mr. Prenty's instructions, Tessa set the white flat-bottomed coffee filter on top of the other cup. She held the edges as Victor poured in the red mushy liquid.

"After most of the liquid has filtered through," Mr. Prenty said, "toss the filter into the food-recycling bin. What's left has the insides of the strawberry cells, including the DNA. To isolate it, we need to change the molecules from a liquid state to a solid one. We'll use rubbing alcohol that's been in the freezer." He held up a couple of white plastic bottles.

When it was their turn, Tessa poured from the ice-cold bottle. The liquid immediately started to separate.

"You can see it's making layers, with the rubbing alcohol on top and the extraction liquid on the bottom. Now gently swirl it." When Victor did, something that looked like cotton fibers started to clump. Mr. Prenty said, "Those white bits are the strawberry DNA. You can fish it out with the coffee stirrer."

As they did, Bree said, "It looks like snot."

Mr. Prenty didn't seem offended. "To our eyes, it does look like snot. But if we could look at it at a molecular level, we would see that classical double helix." With a practiced hand, he drew two linked strands winding around each other like a twisted ladder. "DNA is like a recipe that tells cells how to build an organism. Each of these rungs is like a written step in the recipe."

Tessa regarded the whitish, viscous clump of DNA. She didn't know whether to be impressed or grossed out.

Maybe a bit of both.

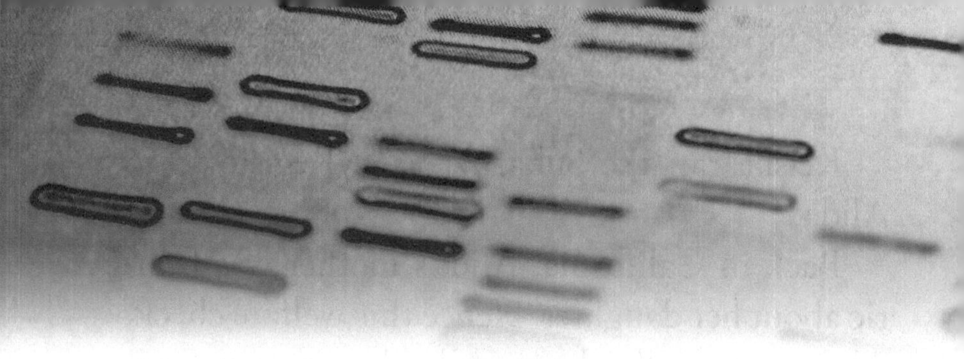

KEISHA

Victim

A WELFARE CHECK ON A TWENTY-TWO-YEAR-OLD was something only an overly anxious mother would demand, Keisha Washington thought as she parked her police cruiser at the curb of the tiny blue house just before noon. The house was rented by Alida Cleary, recent college grad. A ten-year-old maroon Subaru Outback was parked in the driveway.

In Keisha's experience, welfare checks were usually for some old person who would turn out to have died in their sleep, or maybe just fallen and been unable to get up. Not a girl who had probably partied too hard or simply forgotten to charge her cell phone.

Keisha ran the Subaru's plate. Registered to Alida.

Back in California, Alida's mother was frantic about her daughter. Hence this welfare check. Alida supposedly always called home every Sunday at 6 PM but hadn't four days ago. She wasn't answering her phone, and when her mother checked with her employer, they said they had last seen her the previous Friday. Calls to her phone had initially gone to voicemail, which was now full.

Just because her car was here didn't mean Alida was. She could be with a friend or even out for a run. As she got out of her patrol car, Keisha scanned the house. While it needed a coat of paint, there was no gaping door or broken window. She climbed the chipped redbrick stairs.

Her mother had said Alida didn't have a boyfriend. When she had checked with Alida's friends, they hadn't seen or heard from her since Saturday morning.

But in Keisha's mind, everything had asterisks after it. No boyfriend—that her mother knew about. And the friends her mother knew to call were probably not Alida's only friends. Keisha was only three years older than Alida, and Keisha had secrets her parents were never, ever going to find out. So maybe there was a new man—or woman. Or a party had gone on a little too long. Maybe Alida had simply gotten tired of "always."

Keisha pressed the doorbell but heard no corresponding buzz or chime inside. She switched to a sharp knock, loud enough to reach every corner of the house.

Still no footsteps or answering voice. Keisha stood on tiptoe to peep through the row of small glass squares set into the door. A living room with a blue couch, a TV, a brown recliner. No signs of a struggle.

She gave the knob a quick twist. Locked.

Next Keisha circled the house, looking through windows. Living room from a different angle. Tiny dining room. Small, square kitchen with white cabinets and a worn white linoleum floor.

About to move on, Keisha spotted something. The back of her neck prickled. Was that a foot in the kitchen doorway? Or just a random shoe at an odd angle? She pressed her cheek against the glass.

It was definitely a foot, but she couldn't see

more. She knocked on the window, but the foot didn't move.

Was Alida experiencing some type of medical emergency? An overdose?

Keisha keyed her mic and gave her call sign. "Someone's inside on the floor, but they're not moving."

"Ten-four. Be advised, all free units are responding to a twelve-seventy-three on West Burnside."

Keisha swore to herself. If the armed robbery call was legit, she was unlikely to receive backup anytime soon.

Wait! Had the foot just twitched? Keisha knocked on the window again. "Alida? Alida?"

The foot stayed where it was.

Damn it. Keisha remembered the catch in Mrs. Cleary's voice. What if the time it took for backup to arrive was the only time this girl had?

Experimentally, Keisha pushed the sash. It slid up. She keyed her mic again. "Be advised, I'm making entry." Taking a deep breath, she grabbed the frame and scrabbled up and through.

She landed on the balls of her feet, hand on the butt of her service weapon in case things weren't as quiet as they seemed.

But the only sound was her own breathing. She moved toward the body, which had its back against some cupboards.

Because it was a body. She knew it in her gut.

Keisha squatted. Her fingertips pushed past the girl's long dark hair to her throat, already knowing she wouldn't feel a pulse. The girl's skin was cold and firm. Alida was long past saving. Her throat was bruised. Her wide brown eyes stared at nothing.

Alida's blue dress covered her knees. One foot was bare and the other wore a flat her heel had slipped out of. Lying on her chest was a white rectangle. Keisha squinted, resisting the urge to touch it.

A driver's license. But it wasn't Alida's. It belonged to a thirty-two-year-old woman named Rachel Rule.

Keisha's heart stuttered.

Rachel had been the last known victim of the Portland Phantom, two and a half years ago.

TESSA

Knowledge

TESSA GROANED WHEN HER ALARM BUZZED. THEN she remembered. Today she was eighteen, officially an adult.

In the bathroom, she took care with her makeup, making sure her eyeliner flicked up the same on both sides. In her experience, some guys claimed to hate makeup, while at the same time deeming girls wearing tons of it "hot." Victor, who wore a rotating collection of necklaces and single earrings, seemed like he might appreciate her eyeliner both for its artistry and for how it enhanced her eyes.

Tessa pulled on wide-legged flares in her favorite shade of teal, then topped them with a retro-looking, short-sleeved white blouse.

When she walked into the kitchen, Phoebe started singing "Happy Birthday." Her dad joined in from the dining room table, his voice uncharacteristically hoarse, as did her mom from in front of the stove. Normally, they were on their own for breakfast, but birthday chocolate chip pancakes were a family tradition.

When they finished the song, Tessa took a little bow. Dressed in her frog-patterned shorty pajamas, Phoebe began dancing in a circle around Tessa while shaking a small, lumpily wrapped present. "Open it!" she demanded, pushing it into her hands.

Tessa tore off the gift wrap, revealing silver hoop earrings that caught the morning light.

"Oh my goodness, they're beautiful!" She hugged Phoebe, then slid the posts into her ears. Her mom set a plate in front of her. It bore a pancake sort of shaped like Mickey Mouse's head, if you used your imagination.

As her mom sat, her dad got up and left the room, moving slowly. Two weeks before, he had participated in some kind of crazy obstacle race with the word *Warrior* or *Fighter* in the name. While crawling like a snake under strands of barbed wire, he had lost all the skin on his knees. That portion of the course was supposed to be muddy, but he had been at the far end, where it was more like clay.

He returned with a gold-wrapped package a little thicker than a notebook. Tessa's heart started beating faster.

"Happy birthday!" He handed it to her. It had a heft to it. Both her parents were watching expectantly. Lately, they had seemed preoccupied, but this morning their focus was all on her.

Worried it wasn't what she had secretly hoped for, Tessa unwrapped it slowly, ready to fake a smile at the sight of a Kindle.

But it was a MacBook Air. She gasped. She had scooped ice cream at The Creamery all summer, but most of her paychecks had gone for a new phone. Although she had tried to save up for a laptop, there had been new clothes, over-the-ear headphones, and, of course, books.

Tessa hugged the slim box to her chest. The MacBook was by far the most expensive present she had ever received.

"You guys! Really?" For once, she found herself at a loss for words.

"You only turn eighteen once," her dad said. "And you can take it to college next year."

Her mom's voice was choked with emotion. "Remember, no matter how old you get, you'll always be our little girl."

Tessa itched to set it up, but she had only ten minutes before she had to catch the bus. Instead, she hugged her parents and then wolfed her pancake before running out the door.

At school, her locker had been decorated with a blue poster board. Silver glitter spelled out *Tessa* and *18*. A helium balloon was taped above the dial. She twirled the combination, feeling a little embarrassed as passersby offered birthday greetings. El, who had done the decorating, arrived with a chocolate croissant and a hug.

"Lucky you! Now you can enlist in the military!" El gave her a mock salute.

"I think I'll just stick to voting." Tessa spoke around a mouth full of flaky goodness, one hand cupped under her chin.

"You can also rent a U-Haul," El added. "But not a car. Which doesn't make any sense."

"You could do a lot more damage with a

U-Haul," Tessa agreed. "But we don't get to make the rules."

But as she went through the day, it felt like she could. Thanks to El's sign, dozens of people wished her a happy birthday and a few even hugged her. Tessa had always existed in the middle of the popularity bell curve, neither unpopular nor popular, but today she felt noticed and celebrated.

When she took her seat next to Victor in biology, he said, "So today's your birthday? Mine's not until May."

She nodded. "I'm officially an adult now."

Victor leaned in close enough that she smelled whatever kept his thick dark hair from tumbling into his eyes. The scent reminded her of fresh-cut grass. "Happy adulthood, Tessa." One side of his mouth curled up.

Was he flirting with her? Ever since they had become partners, Tessa had noticed how other girls looked at him.

At the front of the room, Mr. Prenty clapped his hands. "Today we're going to be talking about genetic traits. Each table has a vial of paper strips with a small amount of a chemical called PTC. It's harmless to humans. Put a strip on your tongue for a few seconds. Let it get wet, but don't chew or swallow it." He looked meaningfully at Trey.

Victor held out the bottle. Tessa pulled out a white slip and put it on her tongue. He followed suit. Watching his generous mouth made a weird shiver run down her spine. But then bitterness flooded her mouth. The corners of Victor's mouth drew down in disgust. A chorus of "yucks" filled the room, while a handful of people's expressions didn't change.

"Now discard the strip." As they did, Mr. Prenty bounced on the tips of his toes. "What did it taste like?"

"Bitter!" Tessa said, while Victor said, "Nasty!" Others suggested brussels sprouts and old vegetables.

"Like nothing," Bree said.

"Like my mouth tastes the day after a party," Trey said to laughter.

"Like paper," another girl said.

"Raise your hand if you tasted something off-putting."

Tessa scanned the room. Only six people didn't have their hands up.

"About seventy percent of people in North America can taste PTC," Mr. Prenty said. "Children are believed to taste it at a higher frequency. It also varies depending on race. People of African descent, for example, taste PTC at higher frequencies than people of northern European descent."

Trey raised his clasped hands overhead like a boxer who had just won a fight. "I've always said we have a better sense of taste."

"But what good does it do to be able to taste it?" Victor asked.

"Back when humans were hunter-gatherers, it might have made them spit out poisonous roots or berries. The ability to taste PTC is a trait controlled by a single gene. I've been teaching this unit for over twenty years." Mr. Prenty rocked back on his heels. "Back when I started, we'd spend several periods looking at traits like unattached earlobes and widow's peaks—things we believed were controlled by just one gene, like PTC tasting. But over time, we've learned a widow's peak can range from as obvious as Dracula's hairline"—his fingers traced a V on his forehead—"to just a slight dip. Traits usually exist in a range rather than as a binary selection. And almost always, multiple genes are involved. It's similar to how we used to believe two blue-eyed parents could never have a brown-eyed child."

Tessa straightened up. "I thought that was true."

She had read that if you had brown eyes, it meant one of your parents must also have brown eyes. Tessa had hugged that tiny bit of knowledge to herself.

Now, Mr. Prenty shook his head. "That model was too simplistic. Although it's not common, parents with blue eyes can actually have children with brown eyes."

"So science was wrong." Trey crossed his arms.

"Science is always learning. And scientists are willing to let go of old ideas."

Tessa barely heard them. She was still stunned that the single "fact" she'd known about her biological parents had just disappeared.

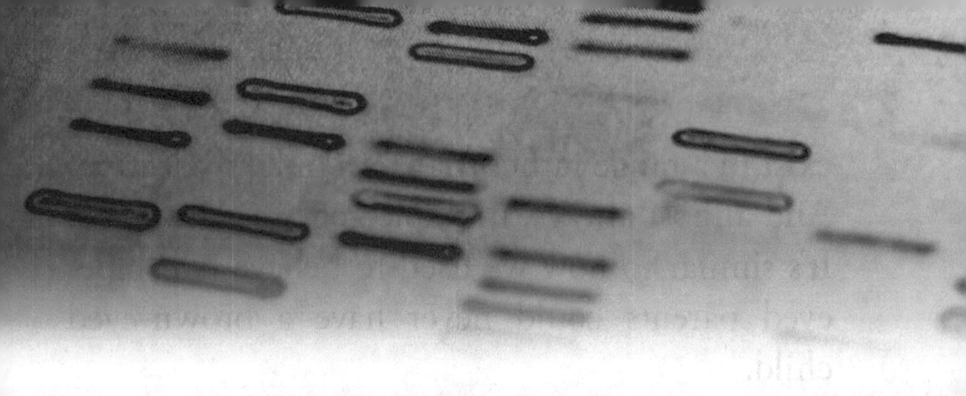

KEISHA

Document

KEISHA WENT UP THE STEPS OF THE GRAY RANCH house across from Alida's little rental.

Yesterday had been a whirlwind. Finding Alida. Recognizing she was past saving. Spotting the driver's license. Realizing this case had just blown up.

Keisha had been debriefed by Shane Morrison, the head of the Portland Phantom task force. It had been two and a half years since the killer had last struck, and as the leads played out, the task force had slowly dwindled. Now it would come roaring back.

And Keisha vowed to be part of that. Somehow. Today she was one of three patrol officers canvassing the neighborhood for witnesses or security camera footage. Canvassing could not only identify suspects but also let frightened residents know the police were doing something.

In this morning's briefing, Alida had been mostly referred to as "the victim." Keisha couldn't think of her so impersonally. She had stared into the young woman's filmed-over eyes. Had helped the medical examiner load her body onto the gurney. Had searched her things with gloved hands. In Alida's bookcase were some of the same books Keisha owned. In the other girl's closet was a black dress Keisha had the twin to. Even though cops were supposed to be like surgeons, impersonal and focused on the problem at hand, Alida's murder had hit home.

When Keisha knocked, she didn't hear any movement inside. People often let a knock go, thinking it was just the Amazon driver. "Portland Police!" she called, and knocked again.

A woman with salt-and-pepper hair answered, one hand on the door and the other on the frame, as if ready to slam it closed. Would that second hand have been there if Keisha was all white instead of half?

The woman, who introduced herself as Mrs. Lanning, finally let her inside. They sat next to each other on an aging green velvet couch that sagged under their weight. Mrs. Lanning looked nervous as Keisha flipped open her notebook and started asking questions.

At first, they were easy. Mrs. Lanning's full name, her date of birth, how long she had lived in the neighborhood. Forty-two years.

In firearms training, Keisha had learned that shooting fast and shooting accurately were usually not the same thing. Despite the urgency, she couldn't rush. If she missed something, she might never get another chance.

She had learned to document everything: location, everyone present, whom she actually spoke with. It wasn't busywork. Information that didn't seem important now might be key later.

They moved on to Alida. Earlier, Keisha had checked her Instagram page. Her profile showed her wearing a daisy crown. When that photo was taken, Alida hadn't known her future. How short it would be. Her broad smile had given Keisha the same unsettled feeling she had seeing photos of murder victims in her homicide textbooks.

When that person had woken up that day, they had no idea they would soon be dead, photographed, a black bar placed over their eyes, their sprawled body displayed to thousands.

Mrs. Lanning had known Alida by sight, waved at her occasionally, and didn't think they had ever exchanged a word. According to the older woman, Alida lived alone, never had more than one strange car in her driveway, didn't throw noisy parties, and seemed like a nice girl.

If Alida had a stalker, focusing on a single day might miss important information. But no matter how she phrased it: "Has anything unusual happened recently?" "Have you noticed any unknown vehicles or strangers?" "Have you heard any unusual noises lately?" she elicited nothing but noes. The older woman's answers lacked the tension of someone lying.

She already guessed the answer from standing on her porch, but Keisha asked it anyway. "Do you have any surveillance cameras, like a Ring doorbell?"

Another shake of the head.

Keisha was reaching for a business card when she remembered to ask, "Do you live alone?" It certainly felt like Mrs. Lanning did, but the rule was you canvassed people, not locations. You couldn't speak to just one person at a residence and check it off your list.

Mrs. Lanning shook her head. "My son lives with me, but he went camping this week."

"What's his name?"

"Chad."

"And how old is he?"

"Thirty-seven."

Keisha's pulse quickened. Chad was much closer in age to Alida. "I'll need to speak with him. When will he be home?" She would interview him as soon as possible, but separately from his mother. People tailored their observations to fit each other, even unconsciously.

And Chad wasn't just a potential witness. As a white male in his late thirties, he was a potential suspect.

QUENTIN

Erase

HIS HANDS RESTING ON HIS DUTY BELT, QUENTIN scanned the crowded bar. It was a quarter to two, a time when nothing good happened, but these college kids were still bouncing up and down under the colorful strobing lights. The orange foam plugs in his ears muffled the noise (it certainly wasn't "music"), but the relentless bass throbbed in his chest like a second heartbeat. The stink of sweat and beer filled his nostrils.

In front of him, three girls were dancing suggestively. Scratch that. Their dress and actions were well past suggestion. Their bodies writhed in ways that made his skin crawl. One girl's tiny crop top was emblazoned with sequins spelling out *Bad Girl.* The girl on her right wore a black skirt so short it could have doubled as a table runner, while the girl on the left flaunted her deviance with a rainbow-colored halter dress. All three wore such heavy false eyelashes their eyes were at half-mast. Well, that, and maybe partially from alcohol, although Quentin tried to keep a lid on any overserving.

His eyes narrowed as the three shimmied and swayed and occasionally ground on one another. Why did they feel the need to put on such a desperate display? These girls, with their reckless behavior and blatant disregard for any sense of decency, were everything he despised.

The old familiar itch started up. So which one deserved to pay for her sins? If he was going to do this thing—and he was not; it was far too soon—which one would Quentin pass the ultimate judgment on? Which would receive the sentence she deserved?

Earlier, Quentin had used the light from his cell phone to check patrons' drivers' licenses as they entered. His little secret was that if a girl happened to appeal to him, he also surreptitiously snapped a picture of her ID.

So he now had a dozen girls' photos, names, ages (unless they were fake IDs, which he rejected out of hand if detected), addresses (although it might be a parental address, not the address of their current dorm or apartment), as well as their heights and weights (unless they had added to the first and subtracted from the second, which nearly everyone did), as well as hair colors (at least the original one) and eye colors (the single probably correct parameter).

While Quentin definitely wasn't going to do anything, just taking a peek wouldn't hurt. Even if you had already ordered, that didn't mean you couldn't look at the menu. Sometime in the next few days, he would go back through the photos and choose a girl to get to know a little better. A dry run, a way to calm his nerves without putting everything on the line.

Everyone thought the Phantom killed strangers. What they didn't understand was that by the time he made his move, he had gotten to know his victim well.

As last call drew closer, the tempo of the club shifted. The once vibrant energy ebbed while the music decelerated into something softer, more intimate. Women gathered their belongings, their earlier vivacity dimming as they prepared to return to reality.

"Excuse me," a voice said behind him. He turned. It was the trio he had been watching. "Could you walk us out to our cars? My mom made me promise I wouldn't take any chances. She's convinced I'm the Portland Phantom's type."

The girl who had spoken wasn't Bad Girl or the lesbian. It was the one in the too-short skirt. Even though Quentin had snapped a picture of her license, of the trio, Short Skirt was the one he was least interested in.

Despite what her mother thought.

The three regarded him expectantly, appealing to the chivalry they assumed came with his black uniform.

"Tanner!" he called out. Tanner was the other bouncer, an off-duty cop. Tanner turned and Quentin patted his chest, gestured at the girls, and walked his fingers in the air. Tanner nodded.

They stepped outside. The cool air was a bracing contrast to the club's sticky heat. Quentin ended up walking side by side with Short Skirt, the other two behind them. Like a stopwatch counting down the time, the women's heels clicked against the pavement as they walked toward the perceived safety of their cars.

"Thank you so much for doing this," Short Skirt said, then stumbled on a broken piece of sidewalk.

Quentin's hand shot out, steadying her. He released just as quickly. "Really, it's no trouble at all."

"My mom's just overprotective. It's ridiculous." She toyed with the outsize silver spiral pin on her left shoulder.

"It's good she cares." And this silly girl didn't appreciate it at all. He had been so distracted by the other two's bids for attention he had forgotten there were more reasons a girl might need to be punished. What about "Honor your father and mother"?

It took only a few minutes to reach the half-empty parking lot. "Here's my car," Bad Girl announced, fumbling in a purse that seemed too small to hold anything of significance. She finally located the keys and held them aloft in triumph. Then she and the lesbian opened the doors to a ten-year-old Toyota, calling goodbyes to Quentin and the remaining girl.

Short Skirt clicked her fob, and a small Nissan a row ahead let out an answering chirp. Quentin walked her to the driver's door. Her friends were already exiting the lot, leaving him and the girl the only people in sight.

"Thanks again." She smiled as she reached for the door handle.

It took a second for Quentin to answer. He was picturing a half dozen possible futures. How quickly he could bundle Short Skirt into the trunk, or knock her unconscious, or put a gun against her ribs and order her to go with him.

With an easy smile, he said, "Of course. Everyone deserves to feel safe."

He gave her a wave as she started the car and pulled out onto the street. His lips moved as he memorized her license plate number. It would make a nice complement to the information he already had from her driver's license.

If this girl was or had been a student, he could also tap into Bridgetown University's online records to learn more. Of course, there were guidelines about taking unauthorized peeks at the data, but Quentin was in charge of monitoring that. He was always careful to erase his cyber footprints.

The same way he did his real ones.

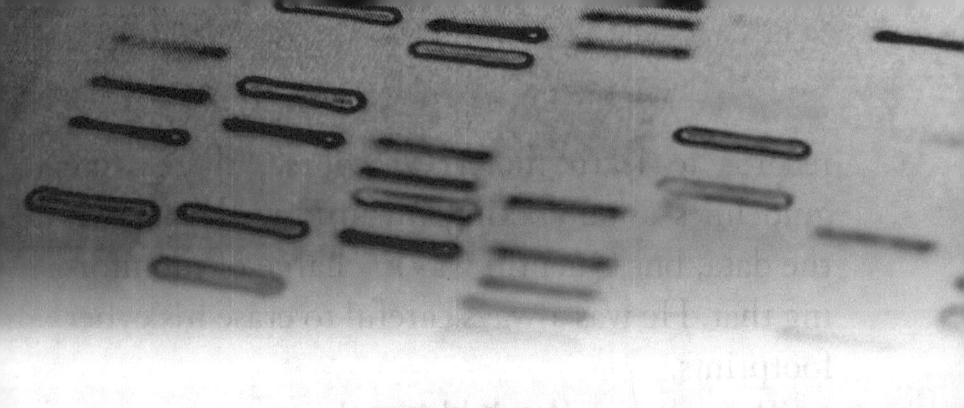

TESSA

Others

WHILE TESSA WAS STILL AT SCHOOL, HER MOM HAD texted, asking her to pick Phoebe up from her after-school program at five thirty and walk her home. Their parents had a meeting at the end of the day. Tessa had the vague impression it had to do with the mortgage. Or maybe taxes. Something stressful and adult.

Now, the older woman sitting behind a battered desk narrowed her eyes at Tessa. "So you're Phoebe's babysitter?" Tessa had never seen her before, so she must be new.

Behind the woman raged the controlled chaos of the after-school program, held in the elementary school's cafeteria. While a few kids were doing homework or coloring, most were playing a game. Phoebe was in the thick of it.

"Boneless!" Phoebe shouted. "Boneless!" Most of the kids slid to the ground, floppy as over-cooked noodles. They would not regain their ability to move until a magical unicorn (a player who had earned enough points) touched them, giving them back their bones.

Tessa knew all the rules because, when she was about Phoebe's age, she had invented the game. It featured unicorns, monsters, safe zones, magical powers, an evil ruler, bouts of bonelessness, and lots of chasing. She had taught it to Phoebe, and it had since spread throughout the after-school program. Phoebe was a natural leader, the extro-vert to Tessa's introvert.

Now Phoebe spotted her. "Tessa!" She ran over and threw her arms around Tessa's waist.

"Phoebe's my sister," Tessa said.

The woman's eyes went back and forth between the two heads, one dark and one fair. This had happened before, with Tessa mistaken for the nanny or the babysitter. Sometimes when she was with her family, she found herself hum-ming *Sesame Street*'s "One of These Things (Is

Not Like the Others).” Only it wasn’t three red balloons and one blue, or three fruits and a shoe.

The thing that didn’t belong was Tessa.

Her eleven-year-old sister was her parents’ surprise biological child. She had the Lundgren look. The Lundgren calmness. Lately, Tessa felt so impatient and moody, especially when surrounded by her family’s unending equanimity. It felt like they had everything figured out, while she was constantly floundering.

Plus, they were all so good at logic and reasoning. Her dad was a mechanical engineer and her mom a CPA. They could all do complicated math in their head, even Phoebe. Phoebe, who got perfect grades and was never, ever moody.

But then Tessa saw how her little sister was looking up at her as if she was the best thing in the world. She forgot her jealousy.

“Come on, let’s go home.” Tessa pulled Phoebe’s pink backpack from a cubby. After she scribbled her name on the sign-out sheet, they left.

Phoebe chattered happily about her day as they walked down the sidewalk. Tessa half listened, lost in her own thoughts. On her new laptop, she had started writing a story about a kitchen wench, an orphan who didn't realize she had secret powers, and her friend the stable boy, a guy who kind of looked like Victor.

Sure, her family understood fractions, clapped on the beat, and thought running was "fun." But did they know the thrill of a story unspooling in your mind, characters who seemed more real than most people, scenes that left even you gasping in surprise? With just a few black marks on white paper, Tessa could transport readers to other worlds.

Or at least transport El. El was always her first, and often her only, reader. El gave just the right feedback. Lots of praise and a few clear suggestions about how to improve things.

Once home, Tessa started dinner. Pasta puttanesca with lots of garlic and kalamata olives. In the freezer, she found some premade garlic bread, and there was a Caesar salad kit in the fridge. None of it was hard, but still Tessa expected some praise when her parents finally came home, ninety minutes later.

Instead, they barely spoke. Barely touched their food.

"Is it too garlicky?" Tessa asked as her mom

scraped most of her dinner into the stainless steel compost container next to the sink.

Her mom's features pinched together. "Tessa, it's not always about you, okay? You don't have to always be the center of attention."

Shocked, Tessa looked to her dad. He glanced up from his plate, which he had barely touched. "We're just tired, honey. It's been a long day."

A lump formed in Tessa's throat, but she swallowed it down. Back in her room, she wrote a new chapter.

The kitchen wench has labored over a feast, including a baked peacock served in its feathers. But the king and queen ignore the masterpiece that has taken her a day of work. And if their liege lords haven't had the first bite, none of their courtiers is allowed to taste it.

Then to everyone's astonishment, the cooked bird gets up, walks down the table, and takes flight.

By the time she finished, Tessa felt a little better. When she set her laptop on her dresser, she remembered the white Ancestry box hidden in the top drawer.

For as long as she remembered, she had felt

incomplete, like a puzzle missing its final piece. Would the parents who had each contributed half of her understand Tessa in a way her adoptive parents didn't?

Who were these people who had given her up? What had stopped them from raising her? Did she have siblings out there? Part of her was terrified to find out. Another part longed to know whose eyes or smile she had inherited. To find people who were like her, the way Phoebe was so like her parents.

And now she had the power to find out the truth about herself.

Tessa opened the drawer.

KEISHA

Away

KEISHA'S CELL PHONE RANG WITH HER WORK RING-tone. The city reimbursed a set amount and you decided how to spend it. Some cops kept their personal and professional lives separate by carrying two phones. Keisha didn't have much of the former.

It was Alida's mom.

"Washington." Keisha kept her tone business-like, hoping it would be catching.

"I've seen you in the neighborhood going door-to-door." Mrs. Cleary had flown up from California, and now that the crime scene—aka Alida's rental—had been released, she was packing up her daughter's things. Even sleeping in what had once been Alida's bed. Although it was hard to imagine she slept much. Keisha certainly wasn't. She'd come home exhausted, but when she closed her eyes, all she saw was the dead girl's face.

"We're canvassing the neighbors, asking if they saw or heard anything."

"Can't you just use DNA like they do on all those crime shows?" Mrs. Cleary's voice cracked.

"The crime scene team was thorough. If he left DNA or a fingerprint or any other clue, they found it." Unfortunately, the killer was an old hand at not leaving anything at a scene. He'd made only one mistake, years ago, and he'd clearly learned from it.

Locard's principle said every criminal left something of himself at the crime scene, and also took something away with him. He might leave behind a fingerprint or a bullet casing. He might take with him dirt from the victim's front yard or a single hair from her head, tangled in one of his buttons.

But what made the Portland Phantom unique was how he deliberately both left and took a souvenir, something small and personal. Yesterday, they had searched for what wasn't there as well as what was. But Alida's earrings (taken from Victim Number Five) were still in her ears, her driver's license (taken from Victim Number Seven) was in her wallet, and her watch (taken from Victim Number Four) was still around her wrist.

"And I know they already asked you, but as you've been going through Alida's things, have you noticed anything missing? Like some jewelry or a scarf? A family photo?"

"I don't see how that helps Alida. It's only going to help you identify the next victim. You need to be working on stopping him. You people have had years to catch him, and as far as I can tell, you still don't know a damn thing about him."

This was the same thing Mrs. Cleary had told all the local news stations last night. Her voice loud and hoarse as she stood on the edge of the lawn, her eyes wild. TV news shows loved angry, articulate people, so she had appeared on not just the local news, but also national and international.

Mothers were mothers. To them, their case was the only case. Although in truth, the news the Portland Phantom had struck again had the entire city on edge.

"That's why we're all working double shifts. That's why I'm going door-to-door today. Science can give us only one part of the puzzle. Sometimes, the old-fashioned methods work best. People may have noticed something without realizing it's important. Then we put all those details together." Keisha added gently, "I promise you, we're doing everything we can."

Mrs. Cleary let out a shaky sigh. "I just want to find out who did this to my baby. She didn't deserve this."

"She didn't. And we've got a whole team working on it. No one will rest until we find her killer."

"Alida has—had—so many friends here. We're going to have a memorial service in Portland Saturday, as well as one back home next Thursday."

This was interesting. "Could you give me the details of the Portland one? We might want to have someone attend."

Mrs. Cleary made a scoffing noise. "The same cops who have been unable to catch this guy all these years?"

"What if it were me?"

There was a long pause, which Keisha didn't rush to fill.

"Maybe."

Keisha acted as if she had said yes. "When and where is it?"

"Saturday at two PM at Chapel of the Bells."

It wasn't unknown for a killer to attend the funeral of his victim, to revel in what he had done. And if he did, Keisha vowed to spot him.

**From the Lifetime documentary
*Chasing Shadows: The Hunt for the Portland
Phantom***

The man on-screen is identified as *Scott Jennings, son of Dana Jennings, the first victim of the Portland Phantom*. Even though he is only in his early thirties, his dark hair is receding, and there are hollows underneath his eyes.

"My mom, Dana, deserves to be remembered as more than just the Phantom's first victim. Even though it was just the two of us, she made sure I had everything I needed. She never missed one of my games. She had this playful, flirtatious side, and it was that warmth that drew people in. The day I came home from practice and found her body was the worst day of my life." He bites his lip. "I lost more than a mother—I lost my best friend."

The camera cuts to narrator Maxwell Holloway nodding gravely. His swept-back hair never moves.

As a photo of Dana Jennings wearing a low-cut red blouse and a delicate gold chain fills the screen, her son says, "She always wore this necklace with her initial *D* on it. It was a gift from my grandma. It was like a part of her, you know? But that day I was too upset to notice it was gone."

The camera shifts to Holloway. "Little did Dana's son know that his mother's cherished possession would eventually become the initial link in the horrible chain law enforcement is still trying desperately to break. Dana's necklace would become the first of the Phantom's eerie calling cards connecting seemingly unrelated victims. And the eventual realization of its significance would lead investigators deeper into the dark labyrinth of the Phantom's world."

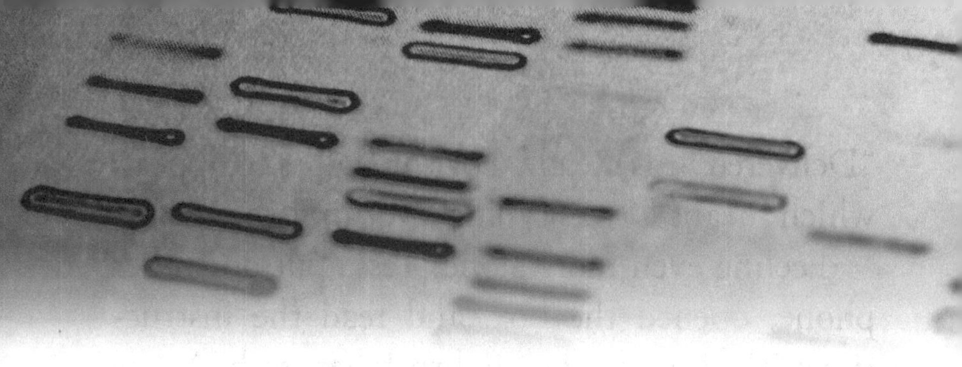

TESSA

Blood

TESSA NEVER LOCKED THE DOOR OF THE BATH-room she shared with Phoebe. Her family obeyed an unspoken rule about bathroom doors. Slightly ajar: available, although someone might be brushing their teeth or applying makeup. Firmly closed: occupied and off-limits.

She wanted no witnesses, and her bedroom didn't have a lock. After thumbing the button on the bathroom door, she took the Ancestry kit from the cardigan she'd wrapped it in. But instead of opening the box, she hesitated.

Tessa texted El. "I'm doing it. I'm taking the test." She waited for the tag to switch from

"Delivered" to "Read." For three dots to appear, which meant El was typing. Nothing changed.

Feeling even more alone, Tessa put down her phone, opened the box, and read the instructions. The first step was to brush her teeth. As she did, she examined her reflected features.

The shape of her eyes, their deep brown color, the dark lashes fringing them—all those came from people she didn't know. Everyone else in this house had pale eyes and stubby lashes. The only time Tessa saw someone with features just like hers—heart-shaped face, full lips, sharply arched brows—was when she looked in the mirror.

What would it be like to be around people who not only looked like her but who also understood her? Lately it seemed like she and her parents were not just on different pages but different planets. Her parents seemed either irritated or distracted, and she kept wondering what she had done wrong.

Earlier in the week, a human-interest story had popped up on Tessa's social media feed. A man even older than her dad had reunited with his birth mother, who had been forced to give him up at sixteen. They had been photographed, grinning, with their heads next to each other. The shapes of their faces and even their smiles had been so alike.

Tessa longed to see herself in another person. To have a connection down to her sinews and bones.

When she was done brushing, Tessa sucked up a palmful of water, swirled it around, and spit it out. The next step was to rub her cheeks against her teeth and gums. As she pressed her cheeks up and down, Tessa watched in the mirror as her pinched-together lips stretched from artificial smile to artificial frown and back again. Underneath the thin layers of skin and muscle, her bones and teeth were hard and unyielding. The skeleton beneath the flesh. Tessa shivered.

After screwing a plastic funnel onto a plastic tube, she was supposed to fill the tube with saliva to the black wavy line. She tried to gather liquid by chewing her tongue and letting the spit dribble out. Finally, she pulled the tube away to check. It wasn't even half done, and it was full of bubbles. The instructions said if that happened, she was supposed to tap it on the counter. When the bubbles settled, she had even less.

If she couldn't produce enough saliva, she could set the tube upright in a refrigerator and try again later. Right! Tessa couldn't imagine the look on her parents' faces if they learned what she was doing. She worked her mouth and tried again.

Someone knocked on the door. Tessa froze.

"I need to pee," Phoebe announced.

Tessa swallowed before she answered, realizing too late she had just lost some of her hard-earned sample. "Go use Mom and Dad's bathroom."

"Mom's in there."

Pieces of the test were scattered all over the counter, and she didn't want to risk messing anything up. "It's going to be a while, Phoebe. You'll probably have better luck asking Mom."

The only answer was silence. Her sister must have left, her feet soundless on the carpet.

Was Tessa making a mistake? Was it wrong to be looking for family when she already had one? She jumped when her phone buzzed. It was a text from El.

"So you're really doing it?"

"When you gave me that test, it was like when

a character in a movie finds a gun. You know it'll be fired before the end."

Three dots appeared, disappeared, appeared again. As Tessa waited, she realized her mouth felt damp again. She drooled into the funnel, and this time when she tapped it on the counter, the spit met the line.

"Are you sure?" El finally answered. "That's kind of a scary example."

Tessa rolled her eyes. First El had given her the test, and now she wanted her not to take it?

"Maybe I'm thinking like that because of the girl who was murdered." That's all everyone at school was talking about, how the Portland Phantom had struck again. "I should go before my parents wonder why I'm spending so much time in the bathroom."

"Okay. See you tomorrow."

Tessa unscrewed the funnel and replaced it with a special cap that held blue liquid. When she tightened it, it released the blue fluid into her sample. As instructed, she shook the tube for five seconds to mix it. Then the tube went into a collection bag, which went into a postage-paid return mailer. She put everything back in the box, wrapped it up in the sweater, and walked out of the bathroom.

The next morning, she dropped the mailer into a mailbox a block from her house. As her fingers released it, she wondered if she was doing the right thing.

QUENTIN

Appetite

THE SHINY RED CAR PULLED INTO THE NO-PARKING zone. Quentin stepped off the curb while pointing at the sign with a slash through it.

The driver, a middle-aged man with slicked-back hair and an air of entitlement, glanced up at him through designer sunglasses. Then he got out of the car and closed the door.

"I'll be here for only a minute, buddy." The car chirped as he locked it. "I'm just picking up my daughter."

Quentin's jaw clenched. "I'm sure if you circle the block a few times, you can find a legal spot. Or try the parking garage. It's just two blocks away." He waited before adding, "Sir."

The man was already walking away. He spoke over his shoulder. "I assume you don't know who I am. James Magellan. The one whose name is on that building. And I'll just be a second."

Quentin raised his voice to bridge the distance. "I could have you towed." Another beat. "Sir."

"And I could have you fired." Magellan rounded the corner.

Quentin clenched his fists and weighed his options. None of them were good. Despite his threat, a tow truck would probably not arrive before Magellan returned. And even if it did, was it worth risking his job to wipe that smug smile off the guy's face?

He forced himself to walk away. Last year, after an altercation with an underage, drunken frat boy whose dad was a vice president at Intel, Quentin had been reminded that just because he was the head of the university's security department, he was not judge and jury. His primary job was to provide assistance: information, directions, access to buildings, escorts late at night. To deal with the occasional theft, assault, or loud party. Not to be "overzealous."

The encounter with Magellan threw off the whole afternoon. Instead of heading straight home, Quentin found himself going to the one place where he could truly be himself. Not a bar, always his father's choice. No, this was a run-down storage complex on the outskirts of town. He had rented it under a fake name, and he had paid five years of rent in cash in advance.

As he got out of his car, Quentin's heart sped up and his palms got damp. This was a risk. But it was also a reward. And for him, nothing was a reward unless it had an element of risk.

The property lacked security cameras, one of the reasons he had chosen it. He still pulled the hood of his sweatshirt over his ball cap and kept his chin tucked.

At Unit 119, he bent down, turned his key in the lock, and pulled the hasp free. No cheap Master Lock for him. He could pick one of those in under fifteen seconds. While any lock could eventually be picked, there was no need to issue an open invitation.

The metal door rattled upward. The first thing he saw—that any random onlooker would see—was the back of the "portable closet" he had bought on Amazon. Meant for clothes storage, it was made of canvas that zipped closed at the front. It was empty, but the canvas back acted like a screen, revealing nothing while sparking no curiosity. He flicked on the lights, then pulled the door closed before stepping around the empty closet to survey his domain.

It was a small space, ten by fifteen. In the middle was his desk and chair, a row of binders lined up along the edge. Along the back wall were two tall white cabinets from IKEA. They had been called Størs, or something like that. The doors were closed, everything nice and neat, a contrast to the stained concrete floor. He went to the cabinet on the right and opened it.

Everyone thought the Portland Phantom took just one thing from a victim, a single clue to display on the body of the next. But that was shortsighted. Why take only one item and then just give it away? So he took at least two, and sometimes as many as a half dozen, depending on what struck his fancy and what there was on offer. One to taunt. The others to remember. To provide a portal to some of the best days of his life.

Ideally, his missions involved plenty of time. Time to rummage through drawers, to search a purse, to consider photos and knickknacks. To stand above the stilled body and admire his work. No one would ever again be annoyed or offended by this broken husk. The media called them victims, but in his mind, they were projects. And like projects, they had a beginning, a middle, and an end. It began when they offended him. The middle section was the longest and in some ways the best: research and planning. And the end, of course, was also the end of them.

On the shelves were Quentin's treasures, one cluster for each project. Earrings, prescription bottles, necklaces, photos, scarves, key chains, name tags, letters. Sometimes he found something he had never taken before, like an artist's paintbrush or a tiny ceramic bluebird.

His most recent display featured the items he had taken from Alida. Her Costco card, a perfume bottle, a locket, and a photo of a younger her with a woman he now knew was her mother. Since everything would eventually be wiped clean, he let himself pick up each object and remember what it had been like to be in her house, slipping from shadow to shadow, searching drawers and shelves for the things that spoke to him. While all the time she lay propped up in the kitchen, finally silent. He had straightened her dress before resting Rachel Rule's driver's license on her chest.

As Quentin regarded his memories made tangible, the tension left his shoulders. While he would have loved to teach Mr. Magellan a lesson, he had to be practical. Better to stick to women, who were smaller. Who could be convinced cooperating might possibly lead to survival.

Quentin could have done what others like him did. Find the disposable and dispose of them. People who lived on the margins, who drew no attention when they disappeared. And while practical, that held no appeal. He focused on those who deserved to be taught a lesson.

Quentin knew he was different from most people. Nature or nurture? Was it his childhood, shaped by abuse, isolation, and illness? Or was the thing that made him different from everyone else in his blood, something he had been born with?

His dad had been a violent man, but in plain

sight. No way would his father have been able to escape detection for eighteen years, the way Quentin had. So had those fists beating him been like a hammer working silver, making him the man he was?

There was no control version of him, no Quentin who had had parents with the energy, time, money, and inclination to give him a good life. This Quentin had created himself.

After admiring the trophies in both cabinets, he opened the drawers on the bottom. They were filled with clothes from Goodwill he used for projects. Because Goodwill operated on a razor-thin margin, donations were put out in the exact same condition as they had been received. There might be coins in a pocket, dandruff on a collar, or even tags from a store. Quentin had several sets of dark pants, dark shirts, even dark shoes. People trying to disguise themselves were usually reluctant to wear someone else's shoes, but not Quentin. If he left shoe prints behind, he wanted them to belong to someone else.

And once he wore these clothes, he would immediately put them back in a donation bin.

So even if he left a fiber behind, it would

never be connected to him. Hair was an even greater risk, now that DNA could be extracted even from a hair without the root. So Quentin kept his head shaved. Everyone thought they understood. A shaved head was the typical line of defense for a guy going bald. But not him. If he did leave a hair behind, it would come from whoever had donated the clothes.

He had slipped up once, years ago. That one stupid girl had scratched him and he hadn't even noticed. He would never make that mistake again.

At work, Quentin had purchased a trace-evidence vacuum. The vacuum came from the company they bought everything else from—caution tape, powerful flashlights, zip ties, and jackets emblazoned with the word *Security*. The company sold to law enforcement as well as private security outfits, but not to civilians. It had been a risk, but he had guessed correctly that no one at the university would go through the invoicing line by line and asked why he needed an evidence vacuum. Now, using it was the last step after he was done with a project.

Quentin always had a few projects in mind.

The more he planned, the less chance he would be caught. The one time he had been spontaneous, it had felt like letting himself off the leash. Exhilarating but also dangerous.

Sometimes it was enough to plan, even if he didn't bring it to completion. To find a young woman, learn everything about her, even walk around her house when she wasn't home and imagine what he could do.

Other times it was enough just to look at his trophies. To remember.

And sometimes all it did was whet his appetite.

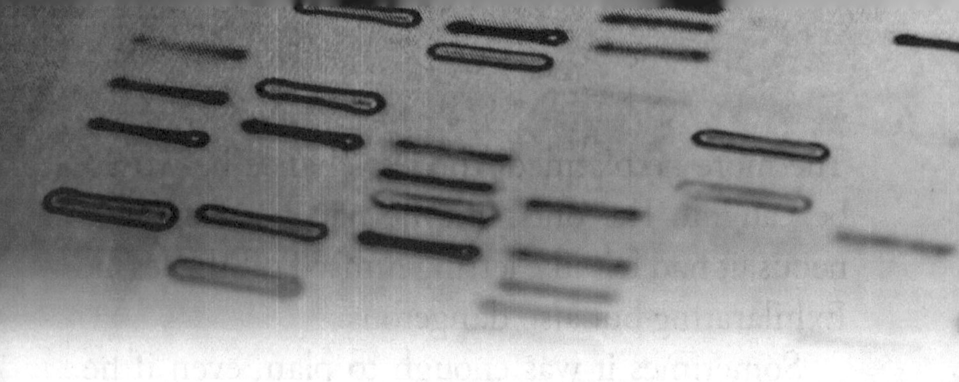

KEISHA

Alarm

CHAD LANNING HAD FINALLY RETURNED FROM HIS camping trip, and now he and Keisha had the Lannings' living room to themselves. No doubt his mother was lurking in the kitchen, listening.

"What did you do the evening of Wednesday the first?" Keisha asked. The medical examiner had said that was when Alida had been strangled.

"I was at Jack's Tavern, and then I came home and went to bed." He looked away. He was about six feet tall and solidly built.

"Did you see any people in or around Alida's house?" she asked. "Any vehicles you didn't recognize?"

He blew air through pursed lips. "No."

"And the next day you went camping?"

"I had a bunch of vacation days coming. This is our slower time of year. Not too hot, not too cold." His face was so tanned his crow's-feet were white.

"And how well did you know Alida?"

Chad leaned back, the creases around his eyes deepening as he considered her question. "Just to say hi to. And a couple of times she showed up at Jack's. Once, we played darts. She was a nice girl."

A nice girl. The statement was so basic it made Keisha suspicious.

"When was the last time you talked to her?"

His eyes shifted. Was he trying to recall or preparing to lie? "Six weeks ago? Maybe a month. We were both in our driveways."

"What did you talk about?"

"Just how hot it had been." Chad rubbed his hands on his thighs. Were they sweating? "Alida didn't have air-conditioning. I said she should talk to her landlord, that I could probably get him a deal."

"So did you look around inside her place to help make an estimate?" A guy who repaired or installed things might also be casing the house or its owner. Dennis Rader, the serial killer known as BTK, had actually installed security systems.

He shook his head. "I've been inside the house before, but not when Alida lived there."

"And how long have you lived here?"

"When I was a kid, of course, but then I moved back home after my divorce. After my dad died, my mom didn't want to be alone." His eyes flicked toward the kitchen.

"When was that?"

"About two and a half years ago."

Keeping her face neutral, Keisha made a note. Around the time of Rachel Rule's murder. Stress was often a trigger for a serial killer. "The bedrooms are upstairs, right? Does your room face Alida's house?"

"Why are you asking me that? I don't watch her or anything." The denial was so swift and specific Keisha automatically reverse engineered the sentence. Chad had watched Alida. Maybe when she was in shortie pajamas or a towel or nothing at all. She might not have been aware he could see her from his second-floor bedroom. Or maybe she had been.

"Have you ever seen her bring anyone home?"

He raised one shoulder and let it fall. "I've seen cars over there, but nobody I paid attention to."

"Did you ever see her arguing with anyone? Do you know if she had any enemies?"

"She was just some girl who lived across the street. Not my best friend or anything." In the kitchen, his mother cleared her throat. "May she rest in peace," he added.

"Why do you think she was murdered?" Keisha put the emphasis on the word *you*, as if Chad had special insight.

"Alida…she was a pretty girl. She was friendly. Maybe she just trusted the wrong person." His eyes flicked to her face as if measuring her response.

That was a plausible theory, but the flat way he said it suggested an undercurrent of bitterness, of being overlooked or ignored. It set off alarm bells.

"Okay." Keisha leaned back in her chair, assessing Chad for a moment longer before standing up. "Remember, if you think of anything else, give me a call." She handed him her card. His hands bore a half dozen small healing scratches. Were they just the natural consequence of his job?

Or something more sinister?

She kept thinking about Chad on the drive back to the station. He would have been nineteen when the first murder happened. Young, but not unheard of. Research into serial killers had found many acted out after a triggering event. Often that was the loss of a job or the loss of love.

How long had his marriage been rocky, putting him under more stress? And living in at least two houses would have given Chad different neighborhoods to become familiar with. Plus, his job had him in and out of people's homes. They needed to look at Chad's job and relationship history, as well as his whereabouts at the time of each murder.

Keisha tried to tamp down the feeling, but what if she were the one? The one who finally caught the Phantom?

TESSA

True

TESSA WAS SURPRISED BY HOW INTERESTING BIOLogy class actually was. Unlike the periodic table or thermodynamics, what Mr. Prenty was teaching actually applied to her own life.

He said, "A length of DNA is divided into segments called chromosomes, and chromosomes are made up of shorter units called genes."

Ancestry had emailed that they were processing her sample and would be in touch once it was done. Now, Tessa checked her email multiple times a day, sometimes even in the middle of class. But all she found was spam.

Mr. Prenty continued, "When people who aren't scientists think about DNA, they are usually thinking about what we call autosomal DNA—the stuff that makes up twenty-two of a person's twenty-three pairs of chromosomes. This is the genetic inheritance you get from both your mother and father."

"My mom's cousin got one of those DNA tests last Christmas," Trey said, "and found out his dad wasn't really his dad."

"That's a little off-topic, Trey," Mr. Prenty said with a sigh. But he must have noticed how the class had perked up. "With those direct-to-consumer tests, you either send in a sample of your spit or a scraping from inside your cheek. Then in the lab, they'll do something similar to what we did with the strawberries on the first day and break down the cells to free the DNA."

"Are they ever wrong?" Tessa stomach's twisted. Victor shot her a sideways glance, as if picking up her stress. "Could Trey's relative's test be wrong about who his dad was?"

With his index finger, Mr. Prenty pushed up his glasses. "There are basically two parts to those tests. One part is an educated guess and the other is highly accurate. When companies claim they can reveal your geographic origin, that's the educated-guess part. If it says your DNA is European or African or Asian, that's pretty solid. If it names a specific country, it may or may not be correct. That part's more recreational science. It shouldn't be taken too seriously, not without paper records to back it up. Their ethnicity estimates are just that: estimates."

Trey straightened up. "So the DNA test *could* be wrong about my mom's cousin's dad?"

Mr. Prenty raised a cautioning finger. "That's the other part of the testing, and the short answer is it's very unlikely. For that, they compare your DNA with that of people who have already submitted samples to their database and look for shared segments. By comparing the length of any shared segments, they can calculate the likelihood of a genetic connection between individuals. Your mom's cousin's DNA should have been about fifty percent the same as the man he thought was his father. So if his mom can't or won't tell him who his biological father is, then he can start looking at close matches and building family trees to see if he can figure it out."

"Why does he even need to build a family tree?" Tessa asked. "Can't he just use his DNA results and find someone who he shares fifty percent of his DNA with?"

"First of all, even though millions of people have done DNA tests, it's still only a fraction of the total population, so he might not have any close matches. Plus, there's more than one testing company, and they generally don't share information, so he would have to test at all of them. And DNA alone can't tell you exactly how you're related to someone, except in very close relationships such as a parent and child. For example, say Trey's mother's cousin shares twelve point five percent of his DNA with someone. That's about how much you would share with a first cousin. But twelve point five percent is also about the percentage you would share with a half aunt or half uncle, or even a great-grandparent."

Victor's eyes flicked upward, like he was calculating. "It's all math. Half, then half, then half again."

"Right." Mr. Prenty nodded. "A DNA test alone can't tell you which of those more distant relationships is the true one. And since men can father children for seventy years, you can't even always use age to rule out a given relationship."

Tessa nibbled a fingernail. Maybe figuring out the identity of her biological parents wasn't going to be as easy as she thought.

She glanced at Victor, who was scribbling notes, his dark eyebrows furrowed in concentration. Victor, who could switch from English to Spanish without thinking. Who wore just as much jewelry as some women even though he was a guy.

Tessa envied how comfortable he was in his own skin. She'd spent her whole life feeling out of place, an impostor in her own family.

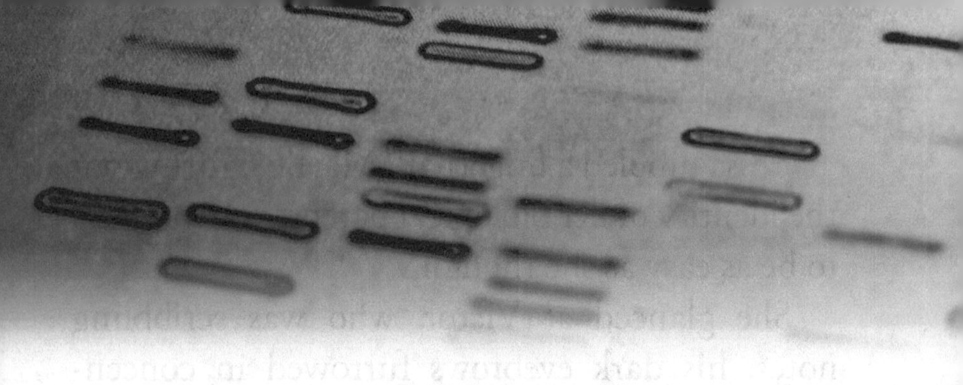

KEISHA

Familiar

WEARING A LONG DARK DRESS AND A BLACK JACKET, Keisha stepped into the Chapel of the Bells. The parking lot was full, so she'd had to park several blocks away and then pass a gauntlet of reporters, ignoring their shouted questions. Most were local, but she'd spotted a couple of faces she recognized from the national news. Alida's murder had pulled the Portland Phantom back into the spotlight.

Even though the funeral was private, the foyer was crowded. Amid the sea of black clothes were splashes of purple—a hair ribbon, a tie, a blouse—which Mrs. Cleary had earlier told

Keisha was Alida's favorite color. Young women wept with their arms around one another. Young men looked tense, with hands balled by their sides and expressions that mixed anger and bafflement. The sprinkling of older folks was probably neighbors or coworkers.

While officers—both plainclothes and not—were stationed outside taking photographs of people and license plates, the Clearys had been adamant no one from Portland Police, except for Keisha, was welcome at the funeral.

Mrs. Cleary stood near the main door to the chapel, surrounded by tearful young women. A tall man Keisha assumed was Alida's father stood behind her, one hand resting on her shoulder. As a girl with a septum piercing gripped Mrs. Cleary's hand and spoke in a low voice, the older woman dabbed her eyes with a crumpled Kleenex. When she caught sight of Keisha, she straightened up and waved her over.

"This is Keisha Washington. She's a detective with the Portland Police Department. And this is Odessa. She and Alida were roommates for three years."

Should Keisha correct Mrs. Cleary about being a detective? But it seemed rude. Instead, she just stretched out her hand. "I'm so sorry for your loss."

The other girl's face contorted as she squeezed Keisha's hand too hard. "If we had still been living together, this wouldn't have happened. But I wanted to move in with my boyfriend."

"Have you spoken with the police about Alida?"

"Not yet." Odessa wiped her nose with the back of her hand.

"Can you give me your number?"

Neither had a pen or paper, so Odessa ended up typing it into Keisha's phone. Afterward, Keisha found a seat in the back. At the front of the room, the closed casket sat behind the podium. It was obscured by flowers. Most were purple.

Scanning the crowd, she spotted some of the neighbors she had canvassed, including Mrs. Lanning and her son, Chad.

Organ music began to play from unseen speakers, and the room soon filled. As the service began, Keisha's eyes kept moving from face to face. A few people looked more curious than mournful. Acquaintances who hadn't known Alida well? Reporters who didn't care about rules as long as they got a scoop?

Or was it possible the Phantom had slipped in with the rest of the crowd?

Maxwell Holloway stands in front of a photograph of a young woman with frizzy brown hair raising a beer bottle. "It was three years before the Portland Phantom struck again. His second victim was twenty-one-year-old Candy Rossner, a Bridgetown University student who opted to stay behind in the quiet dorms over Christmas break. The grim discovery of Dana's missing necklace on Candy's lifeless body would later prove to be a pivotal clue, although the out-of-place jewelry was initially overlooked by investigators. In addition to fastening Dana's necklace around Candy's neck, the killer took her pink beret as well as her life."

Holloway's voice lingers on the word *life*, seemingly relishing the drama of it.

"When Candy's battered body was discovered, it was clear a violent struggle

had occurred. But Candy had managed
to leave investigators a crucial clue. She
had scratched her assailant, leaving a
tiny bit of DNA under her fingernails.
This first breakthrough was also the last.
Unfortunately, no match for her killer's DNA
was found in the CODIS database."

KEISHA

Chance

KEISHA TOOK A DEEP BREATH BEFORE SHE KNOCKED on Sergeant Gomez's door.

"Come in," his deep voice called out.

Sergio Gomez swiveled in his chair as she closed the door behind her. He had a lined face that always looked tired. He hated small talk, unless it was about his beloved Portland Timbers and Thorns soccer teams.

"I'm reporting back about Alida Cleary's funeral."

"And?" He tilted his head.

"She was well-liked, just like her mom said. Lots of friends. There were a few people the mom didn't recognize, but when she asked around, they were from Alida's work or friends the mom hadn't met yet." She took a breath. "Mrs. Cleary made it pretty clear she thinks we're falling down on the job. After the service, she wanted to go storming out to the press just like she did the other night."

He pinched the bridge of his nose.

"I managed to talk her out of it. She was flying home last night, so hopefully that's the end of it." The more Mrs. Cleary said they were incompetent, the less people would want to cooperate.

His shoulders loosened. "Well, that's good news. I don't need the media speculating and second-guessing any more than they already are. Nor do I need the community more on edge."

Keisha took a deep breath. "So, um, I was wondering if it would be possible to join the task force?" In her head, she cursed herself. Why did she sound so uncertain?

He was already shaking his head. "I need you back on patrol. Especially now that we're getting so many calls from nervous civilians."

She was risking getting on his bad side, but she forced herself not to back down. "But you're going to be staffing it back up again, right?"

He shrugged and picked up some paperwork,

as if signaling this conversation was at an end. "We do need to add more people. But we've got officers with lots more experience. You've been on the force for—how long?"

"A year." Keisha rounded up. It had actually been ten months.

He didn't say anything, as if she had answered her own question. But he also hadn't exactly said no.

She tried again. "Maybe being younger is a good thing."

"Because you'll see things with 'fresh eyes'?" He made air quotes with his free hand.

"Well, that, but I'm also about the same age as the victims. And I'm female. You've got what—two women on the task force? Both in their late forties? We need to understand the victims to understand why this guy chose them. He's not spontaneous. He plans. And as someone the same age and gender as the people he picks, I might have more insight into why he is choosing these particular victims."

He started to shake his head just as there was a knock on the door. It was Detective Bryce Samuels, a beefy guy whose head was basically a cube. "Sarge, we've got a situation."

"What's up?"

"Alida Cleary's mom is on the street outside. And she's shouting."

"What?" He raked his fingers through his graying hair. "I thought she was going back to California." He shot Keisha a look.

"All I know is that she's out there with a big poster with her daughter's face. It says, 'Why can't Portland Police find the Phantom?' She's telling anyone who will listen—and right now, Channel Eight is already parking their mobile unit—we can't be trusted. That if we haven't found the Phantom by now, we never will."

Sergio pushed back his chair. "I'll go down and talk to her."

Keisha saw her chance. "Let me. I already know her. She likes me."

He made a scoffing noise. "If she likes you so much, why didn't she tell you she was going to pull this little stunt?"

"She must have changed her mind. But what if I can get her to stop? Would you"—Keisha hesitated, not wanting Bryce to hear her idea if it was going to be shot down—"think about what I said?"

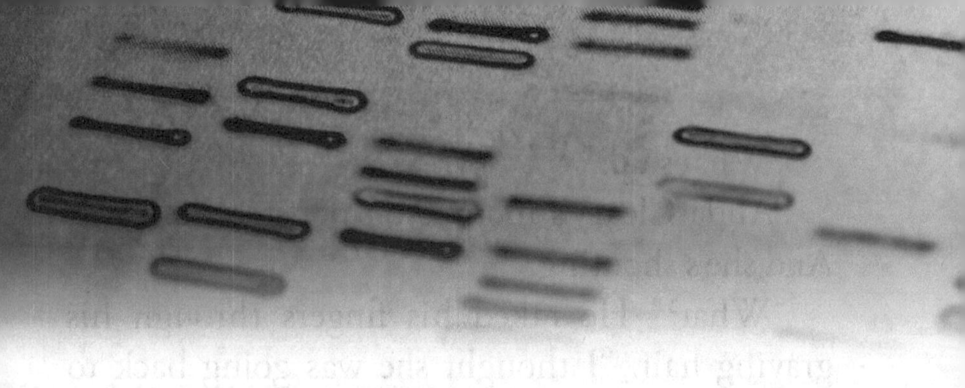

TESSA

Child

TESSA AND EL WERE DEEP IN CONVERSATION IN THE cafeteria when a voice interrupted her.

"Can I join you for lunch?"

Tessa looked up. It was Victor. After two weeks of being lab partners, she felt perfectly comfortable around him in biology. But it felt strange to be interacting with him in the crowded cafeteria. Was everyone looking at them?

Of course, she had already checked out where he normally sat, which was at the table closest to the windows. Most of his friends didn't fit into any one slot. A few were athletes, but track-and-field, not football. Some were artists, others in the tech club, and a handful were musicians. Not the most popular, but not outcasts either.

El gave Tessa an almost imperceptible nod. "Sure," she said, scooting over. "El, this is Victor, my biology partner. Victor, this is El, my oldest friend."

"I like your hair," he said, threading his long legs over the bench seat. El's hair was pink today, and not a soft pink, either, but a saturated Barbie pink.

"Thanks." El nodded.

"So how long have you guys known each other?" Victor asked.

"Since third grade," El answered.

Should Tessa do this? Should she tell Victor how they became friends? Figuring out where she'd come from was all she thought about these days.

She took a deep breath. "El stood up for me when the substitute teacher assigned us to do a family tree over Thanksgiving."

"Why would El need to—" Victor started, then paused, a forkful of coleslaw halfway to his mouth. Squinting, he cocked his head to one side. "Does that have anything to do with all your questions about heredity and genetics?"

El looked impressed.

The words tumbled out of Tessa. "Right after I was born, someone left me at a fire station, wrapped in a flannel nightgown. No note or anything. No clues to my biological parents. But now that I'm eighteen, I can do a DNA test and maybe figure it out."

Victor chewed thoughtfully. "So are you going to do it?" he finally asked.

"Already did." Tessa spoke with a confidence she didn't feel. "Just waiting for my results." She pushed away her plate. The food she had eaten suddenly felt like a rock in her stomach.

"But there's two parts to that, isn't there?"

"You mean ethnicity and DNA matches?" Tessa asked, thinking back to what Mr. Prenty had told Trey.

"That's not what I meant. It's not just about learning who they are or were, right?" Victor's voice was so soft Tessa had to lean forward to hear him over the clatter of silverware and the chatter of other students. "It's also going to mean learning why they left you there." His dark eyes were full of sympathy.

■ ■ ■ ■ ■ ■

Late that afternoon, Tessa sat in her orange chair, the MacBook open on her lap. Her fingers rested on the keys, but the screen showed nothing more than a blinking cursor.

Finally, she started typing.

> "Hi, I'm Sarah," the young woman said tentatively, her eyes searching the careworn face of the woman who had just answered the door. "I've spent my whole life wondering about you. I think you might be my biological mother."

Tessa stared at the screen for a long time. But instead of writing what came next, she put her finger on the backspace key and held it down until it went from deleting individual letters to gulping whole words. She only stopped when the screen was blank.

After a few minutes, she tried again.

> Grace looked at the man sitting across
> from her in the small café. His face was
> weathered, and his salt-and-pepper hair
> reached his collar. She squeezed her hands
> together, trying to quiet her nerves. "Dad,"
> she began, her words catching in her
> throat. "I've been wondering about you
> my whole life."

Tessa sighed and backspaced again until everything disappeared. She couldn't stop thinking about the look in Victor's eyes. He had forced her to acknowledge that she had been thinking about her past the way a child would. But she wasn't in third grade anymore. Her bio parents were not going to turn out to be rich and famous and talented. They probably weren't still going to be a couple. They might not welcome her with open arms.

They might not want to know her at all.

What had she done? Couldn't she just be happy with the parents who had chosen her instead of rejecting her? The parents who would never, ever give her up?

With another sigh, Tessa closed the laptop and set it aside, then went downstairs. She frowned at the sight of Phoebe sitting in front of the TV while also looking at her phone, which their parents had allowed her to get at the beginning of the school year. They were big about limiting screen time. Right now, her mom and dad should be making dinner together and Phoebe should be lost in a book.

She walked down the hall to their room. The carpet muffled her footsteps, but her parents' words were clear through the closed door.

"I'm sick of how you are always looking at me like that now," her dad said. He wasn't a yeller, but his voice was definitely raised.

"Like what?" her mom snapped.

"Like you've already given up on me."

Their words sucked all the air out of the hall. Tessa turned and fled back to the living room. When her parents emerged from their room five minutes later, she was curled around Phoebe. Her eyes were fastened on the TV, but she saw nothing.

KEISHA

Artist

IT WAS 11:17 PM AND KEISHA WAS STILL SITTING IN the conference room she had entered at 8 AM, when she had met the other thirteen members of the task force. She had earned her place by talking Mrs. Cleary out of her one-woman protest. It hadn't been easy, but Keisha saying she would be joining the task force had mollified the older woman.

When the day had begun, Keisha had been nervous, but a meeting was still a meeting, full of droning reports and details and subtle jockeying for power. It had been a bit disappointing to find out the software the task force used was not some supersecret, crime-fighting technology, just off-the-shelf database-management software. Only, instead of using it to inventory widgets, they were tracking the darkest crimes imaginable.

And the room's whiteboards weren't covered with sales projections, but photos of bodies. Some from a distance, while others were close-up photos of a bruised neck or one of the killer's calling cards: a small trophy that had proved to be from a previous victim.

Keisha had mostly listened, although at one point she reported on her interview with Chad. The two other female task force members had quickly let the air out of her enthusiasm. Lori, who talked with her hands as much as her mouth, had explained serial killers usually stayed close to home for their first kills and ventured farther afield as they gained more experience. And Dana, the first victim, would have been a thirty-minute drive from where Chad was still going to high school. Her tone had been only mildly patronizing. Jessica, whose blond bob was an aggressive shade of platinum, had rolled her eyes.

In Keisha's experience, other female officers were less inclined to offer support or guidance than her male counterparts. Maybe women worried they would look soft if they were nurturing, or maybe they just perceived Keisha as competition.

It was late afternoon when the task force adjourned. Keisha had stayed behind to read the murder books. There was one for each victim, and each "book" was actually a series of blue binders filled with information about the victim, the crime, suspects, leads, tips, interviews, and pathology reports.

"Keisha?" a voice said behind her. "What are you still doing here?"

It was Shane Morrison, the head of the task force. His salt-and-pepper hair was so short it bristled. His suit was rumpled, but it had looked the same fifteen hours earlier.

She set her white plastic spoon next to the Styrofoam cup of instant ramen that was her dinner. "Reading the murder books." It had been hard not to think about how these women were not much different from herself.

"What are your thoughts on the victimology?"

Was he testing her or did he really want to know? Victimology was a close examination of the victim, their age, occupation, personality, habits, actions, vulnerabilities, physical characteristics, and whereabouts before the crime. When Keisha had first come across the term in a criminal-justice class, it had seemed like victim blaming. But now it made sense. A victim was chosen for a reason. Understand the why, and you might figure out the who.

She was too tired to be nervous or overthink things. "All the victims have a similar look, with that long hair. A similar age. All women, or female identifying."

"The killer might not have known Passion Flower was trans until he learned it from the media," Shane said. "Even the medical examiner was surprised when he undressed the body." He tilted his head. "What else have you noticed?"

"There's no overkill. The victims really don't have any other injuries past strangulation. That points to them being strangers, not someone he had an emotional connection with. He also doesn't bother to cover their faces or hide their bodies. He doesn't feel guilty. I would guess he feels contempt for the victims, maybe even a disdain for women in general."

Shane said, "What about the fact he doesn't sexually assault them?"

Keisha blew air through pursed lips. "But sexual assault isn't about sex. It's about power. And what's more powerful than murder? He could be targeting women because they're generally smaller and weaker, or because he's angry at women in general."

After a pause, Shane nodded. If this was a test, Keisha felt like she was passing.

"He's organized, which means he probably stalked each victim beforehand, getting to know their schedules." She tried to suppress a shiver. "He's comfortable taking life. And not at a distance, but up close and personal. Maybe he was in the service?"

Shane rested his hip on the table. "There's been speculation he may have served or had some sort of interest in the military or law enforcement."

"Strangulation is not as easy as people think, so he's strong. But looking at the autopsy reports, he's not bludgeoning or tying up these women beforehand. Maybe he uses a gun to subdue them until he can get his hands around their throat. But I think in order to get close to them, he's feeding them a line, or he's good-looking, or he has the gift of gab—something that makes them drop their guard."

"Go on."

"He lives in Portland. He's killing at different times, so he's not a blue-collar worker who always has to be in a certain place at a certain time. His job might have flexible hours or allow him to move around the city easily." Keisha ticked off possibilities on her fingers. "Maybe a gardener. A delivery driver. A handyman. A real estate agent. A Lyft driver." She paused. "Or, like Chad, someone who installs something."

Shane made a noncommittal noise she took as encouragement.

"He's good at what he does, and every time he doesn't get caught, he feels empowered to do it again."

Shane's sigh was long and deep. "I've been on this task force since Candy Rossner was killed and we realized she was actually the second victim. I've been leading it since Passion Flower was murdered. Do you know how many times I've gone through this process? It makes you feel helpless. Hopeless. You go in thinking you're going to solve it, but when you don't…" For a minute, his words hung in the air. "You're doing the right thing." He leaned forward and tapped the tall stack of blue binders. "There's an old saying: 'To know the artist, study his art.'"

A photo of a thirtysomething woman wearing heavy false eyelashes appears on the screen behind Maxwell Holloway. In his gravelly baritone, he says, "Even after Candy Rossner was murdered, her killing was seen as a one-off. Police had yet to link her death with that of Dana Jennings.

"But everything would change after the murder of Kylie Williams, a thirty-six-year-old escort. She was strangled, the same fate that had met the previous two victims."

On-screen, the photo of Kylie is replaced by a photograph of a pink beret next to an evidence ruler.

"But a mysterious twist emerged when Kylie's roommate said she had never seen the pink beret the dead woman was wearing. The beret bore the unexpected

DNA of Candy Rossner, leading to her being identified as another of the killer's victims. The revelations didn't end there. Detective Shane Morrison then connected the necklace bearing the initial *D* found on Candy's body to Dana Jennings, the first victim."

Detective Morrison appears on-screen. "I couldn't help wondering what item from Kylie would turn up on the next victim. Because at that point, I knew there would probably be a next victim." He sighs. "Unfortunately, the media learned about the killer's calling card. It was clear that he was both claiming these murders and rubbing them in our faces."

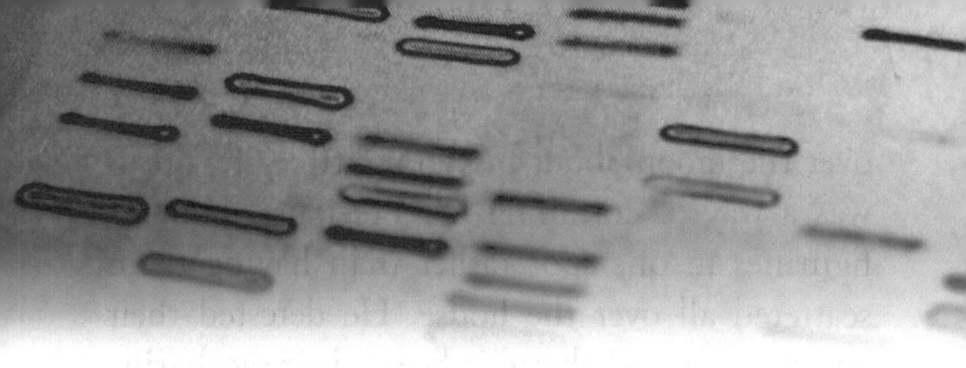

QUENTIN

Precious

WHEN QUENTIN WALKED IN, MELANIE TURNED OFF the TV and got to her feet. She gave him a hug.

"I need your help." Pulling back, she looked up at him with her large blue eyes. Her waist-length brown hair was pulled back into a pony-tail. Even now that she was in her late thirties, if Melanie ordered a glass of white wine, she might be asked for ID.

"With what?"

As he spoke, Quentin set his duty belt next to the large curio cabinet. From the glass shelves, hundreds of teardrop-shaped black eyes regarded him. Quentin had bought the display case two years ago for Melanie's birthday. She had been over the moon about his thoughtful gift, but it was a way of corralling her Precious Moments figurines in one spot rather than having them scattered all over the house. He detested their pastel colors and cherubic faces, their saccharine depictions of joy and innocence. They were part of his wife's world, not his.

But on balance, having a gold ring on his finger and a wife at home was good for Quentin. By the time you were his age, a guy who hadn't settled down was suspect. Melanie washed his clothes, made his meals, and never asked too many questions.

She went into the kitchen and pulled two bowls from the fridge. "I need you to taste test." She handed him a fork. "Which potato salad should I take to the church picnic?"

Quentin regarded them. One was creamy with mayonnaise, the way he liked it. The other had unpeeled yellow potatoes and no visible sauce, just scattered tiny yellow dots. But a sauce made any dish better, which was why a bottle of ketchup was always on the dining room table.

Just to get it over with, Quentin reluctantly forked up a bite of the second one. Sourness spread over his tongue. "What's in that?" He forced himself to chew and swallow, grimacing as the tiny balls broke between his teeth.

"Vinegar and mustard seed. I thought it'd be a fun little play on words."

"Yeah?" He poked the fork tines into a potato from the first salad.

"If you shall have faith as small as a grain of mustard seed," Melanie recited, eyes shining, "you will say to the mountain, 'Move from there to here, and it will move.'" Her hand went to her blue-flowered dress and pressed her flat belly.

Quentin regarded her for a long moment. Her hopeful gaze never wavered. Initially, that spark of naivety had drawn him in. Now it made his skin itch.

"Have you ever heard of a mountain moving just because someone wished it?" he said roughly.

The smile fell from her face. Three years ago, she had asked if they could go to a fertility specialist. After all, they had been married for twelve years. Shouldn't they have had a baby by this time? Her coworker at the fabric store had gone to a specialist and now had a six-month-old.

Quentin had said no. If God wanted them to have a child, he told her, they would.

Since then, she had prayed and prayed for a baby, but none had come.

Nor, to his shame, would it. What kind of a man couldn't sire a child, something every stupid, drunken kid Quentin had kicked out of a bar was capable of? If people—especially Melanie—knew the truth, in their eyes he would become less of a man. He was strong like a man and could fix anything mechanical. But real men were virile, and he could never be a father. He might look like a man, but when it counted, he could shoot only blanks.

So when that girl tried to pin her mistake on him, he had known immediately she was lying.

His childhood was a time Quentin never spoke of and tried not to think about. His father was unpredictable. One moment, he would be laughing and joking; the next, his face would darken, his eyes narrowed into slits. It could happen if Quentin spilled his milk, if he did not jump to obey a command, or for no reason at all.

One of his earliest memories was of hiding while his father raged drunkenly through the house. His dad liked to throw things or put his fist or foot through them. Crush anything small and precious beneath his heel, sweep his arm across a table, hurl a dish at your head. His dad saw the world as being filled with things begging to be broken.

When Quentin was five and bruises bloomed on his skin, his mother thought they had come from his father's fists, the way hers had. Then one bath time, she took off Quentin's shoes and socks and found his feet purple underneath. She tried to rub the color away, but it stayed.

When she took him to the doctor, she dressed in long sleeves and a high neck. The way she always dressed when she went out in public.

The type of leukemia Quentin was diagnosed with was called ALL, and to his young mind, that made sense. It seemed bigger than everything. He had almost died from it, then almost died from the treatment. Everything the doctors tried failed, until finally only one option was left. A bone marrow transplant.

He didn't remember much, which was a blessing. They had to nearly kill you to save you. He'd been in the hospital for two months, weak for a year afterward. A year of no visitors, of limited diet and strict hygiene, even a special air purifier in his room. His immune system had to rebuild itself from the new healthy marrow. A hospital volunteer had given him a donated educational toy that looked like a primitive laptop, and it was then his love of computers had begun.

His dad had been ashamed of his weakling son with bad blood. He was their only child. Both his parents were children of immigrants, never quite at home wherever they were.

When Quentin was thirteen, his father was beaten to death in a bar fight. There was no grief, only relief tinged with anxiety of an uncertain future. His mother had taken on two jobs to keep them afloat.

Only after his father was dead did she reveal that the chemotherapy and full-body radiation Quentin had undergone meant that while he would have a normal testosterone level, he would probably never make sperm. He had been so embarrassed that it was only after he was alone that he realized he would never be able to have a child. The knowledge had changed something inside him. And when he married Melanie fifteen years later, he never told her the truth.

He never told her a lot of things.

The world was cruel. It had denied him the simple pleasure of seeing his own child.

Now, as he lifted another spoonful of the good potato salad toward his mouth, he felt an unexpected rush of guilt. He regarded Melanie's slumped shoulders and thought about the baby she would never have.

"I love the creamy one," he said. "That's what you should take. Everyone's going to be fighting over it."

As Melanie's face brightened, Quentin resolved to go online later and buy her another Precious Moments figurine. Maybe one of the retired ones. In an original box.

KEISHA

Fire

AFTER KEISHA KNOCKED, ODESSA OPENED THE door to her duplex. Keisha had suggested meeting here, hoping to make Odessa comfortable opening up about her old friend.

The small living room smelled of coffee and incense. Keisha took a padded wooden chair that might have once been part of a dining room set, while Odessa settled onto a gold patterned love seat also showing its age.

"So what do you want to know about Alida?" Odessa tucked her brown hair behind her ears, revealing a series of silver studs set along the cartilage. Small tattoos decorated her arms and even the backs of her hands. Keisha didn't remember them from the funeral, but they might have been covered with foundation. Young women their age were good at choosing what to present.

Had Alida been the same? One person at work, another to her parents, a third to her friends?

"How long did you and Alida know each other?"

"We met freshman year in the dorms. We lived next door to each other, but we ended up liking each other way more than we liked our assigned roommates, so we switched."

"Can you tell me more about what Alida was like?"

"Outgoing. Vibrant." Odessa closed her eyes for a long moment. "She'd walk into a room, and suddenly it would feel warmer and brighter. Alida was the kind of person who could start talking to a stranger in the grocery store line and by the time her groceries were bagged, they were friends. She just had this energy about her." She twisted the silver ring on her left thumb.

"Did she get along with everyone?" Keisha asked.

Odessa snorted. "She was no pushover, and some people, especially guys, don't like that.

She didn't start arguments, but if someone else did, she would not back down. And she couldn't stand bullies."

"Did she ever feel nervous, like someone was following her? Or can you think of anyone who made her uncomfortable?"

"No." Odessa drew the word out. "I think she felt safe at that little house. She might have let down her guard. Maybe she even knew the guy from someplace else."

"Didn't you say you used to live with her?"

"Yeah. I moved out six months ago to live with my boyfriend." She blinked rapidly and ran the knuckle of her index finger under one eye. "Maybe if I had stayed put, none of this would have happened."

"That's a one-bedroom house," Keisha observed in a neutral tone.

"The couch turns into a bed," Odessa said, but something made Keisha tilt her head. After a second, she added, "That's what we always told our parents."

"So you were more than just friends?"

Odessa's mouth twisted, but her eyes were steady. "Sometimes we have been."

"Was it over when you moved in with your boyfriend?"

"Not all the time, no. He knew about it and he didn't mind."

"How old is he?" Keisha asked, suddenly wondering if the boyfriend did mind, if he minded very much. Maybe the Phantom was hunting close to home.

"Twenty-five."

The idea was gone as fast as it came. "So why do you think he chose Alida? Because we believe he chooses his victims. Maybe weeks or even months in advance."

Odessa took a deep breath. "I think he saw her, saw her fire. And he wanted to put it out. He wanted to show he was the one in control." Her eyes hardened. "But he can't erase what she was. Alida was a beacon of light."

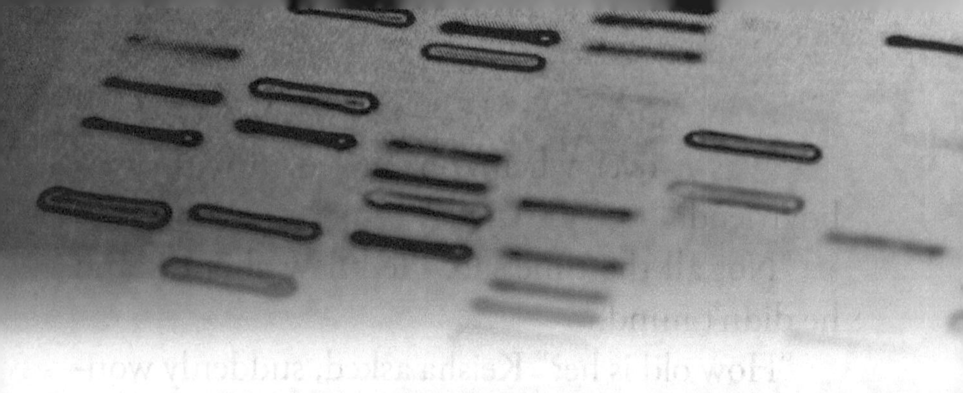

TESSA

Buried

TESSA SPRAWLED ON HER BED, SCROLLING THROUGH Instagram on her laptop without really seeing the carefully composed photos. Refreshing her email wouldn't make her Ancestry results come any faster, but she still succumbed to the urge to check again.

The subject line of the top email read: *Your AncestryDNA Results Are In!*

She hesitated. Once she clicked, she couldn't go back. Tessa tried to imagine her parents' faces, their hurt and disappointment. She didn't even have to imagine. Ever since she had overheard them arguing, she had become aware of how seldom they smiled these days, and how fake it looked when they did.

And if they found out about this, wouldn't it make things worse?

Then again, whatever was wrong was about them, not her, and it wasn't like they were saying anything to her about it. Phoebe was too young, but Tessa was old enough—after all, she was eighteen now. Her parents could at least give her a heads-up if they were getting a divorce.

And didn't Tessa have the right to know her own story?

After taking a deep breath that did nothing to calm her racing heart, she clicked on the email.

At the top was a colorful pie chart with many slices: Irish, Portuguese, Spanish, Welsh, Italian, French, English, Scottish, and more. The largest accounted for only 13 percent of her genetic makeup.

Not two to three ancestries, the way she had always imagined, but close to a dozen. Mr. Prenty had called this part of the test an educated guess, but still it seemed clear Tessa was never going to be able to claim a certain special dish, costume, or type of music. Not like the genetic Lundgrens, with their soft lefse flatbread, sweet brown gjetost cheese, and bright red- or blue-embroidered wool costumes worn over snowy white shirts.

Tessa was a mutt, not a purebred. She steadied herself. Everyone knew mutts were stronger than purebreds. Maybe instead of seeing her ethnic heritage as a random mess of threads, she should view it as an intricate tapestry.

She kept scrolling. Past the pie chart was a section labeled DNA Matches that said "400+ fourth cousins or closer." She clicked. A long list appeared. The first page of results showed only outlines of heads—blue for males and pink for females. Some had full names, some initials, some a mix of letters and numbers. The top one, which was the closest match, said "1st-2nd Cousin, 480 cM | 7% shared DNA."

Tessa tore her eyes away long enough to pick up her phone and text El. She couldn't do this by herself, not the scientific parts and especially not the emotional parts. "Ancestry results in. Can you come over?"

El responded within seconds. "Yes!"

Tessa switched back to her laptop and looked

closer at her highest match, which was pink and labeled "ARS." Other tags read "Parent Two" and "Public linked tree with 8 people" and "Do you recognize them?" with yes and no buttons.

How Tessa wished she could click yes. What did the *A* stand for? Anita? Andrea? Autumn? How old was ARS? Did ARS know about Tessa? Could she at least offer more hints? How could Tessa get in touch with ARS, and if she did, what should she say?

After opening another browser window, Tessa googled first and second cousins. First cousins were just regular cousins, sharing grandparents. Second cousins shared great-grandparents. Her three remaining adoptive grandparents were in their late seventies or early eighties. Their parents must have been born more than a hundred years ago, a time before television, let alone DNA and the internet.

Her probable relationship with ARS was also a link. Tessa clicked. It said there was an 89 percent chance ARS was her first cousin, once removed. What did that even mean? It also listed other, less likely possibilities: half first cousin, great-great-aunt, and great-great-niece.

There was also a 4 percent chance ARS was her great-grandmother, great-grandchild, half aunt, half niece, great-aunt, or great-niece. It reminded her of Mr. Prenty's explanations, only this made even less sense. Victor had said the numbers were "just math," but it didn't seem that simple.

In fact, it was overwhelming. Tessa wanted to slam the laptop closed. Downstairs, the front door opened and El's voice called up. "I'm here!"

"Come on up!"

A few seconds later, her bedroom door opened. Tessa's face must have given her away, because the first thing El said was "What's wrong?"

"I guess it was wishful thinking to hope Ancestry would say who my parents were. I mean, it says I have over four hundred matches, but I don't even know where to start." Each one felt like a mystery that had to be solved before Tessa could know her own secrets.

El sat on the bed next to her. "Start from the beginning."

And when Tessa did, just explaining helped make things clearer to herself. Like could this ARS person actually be her great-great-aunt? That was three generations different. It might be mathematically possible, but not reality possible. Having a great-great-niece was even more ridiculous, since, of course, she wasn't old enough to have a regular niece. By the time Tessa had a great-great-niece, she would probably be dead and buried.

A shiver crawled over her skin. She and El had dreamed up so many possible versions of parents for Tessa.

But they had never once considered the possibility her parents were dead.

"Murder is a big step, even for a highly deviant mind," says a woman identified as psychologist Dr. Evelyn Thornfield. "Initially, the perpetrator himself may be shocked by his own actions. He starts to obsess about his deeds. But eventually memory is not enough, and he feels he must kill again."

Maxwell Holloway's signature eyebrows rise. "How hard is it to identify a serial killer?"

"In everyday life, serial killers do not look or act like monsters. If they did, it would be much easier to catch them. It is not uncommon for the neighbors to say the killer was the last person in the world they would have suspected. They will say how quiet he was, meek, kept to himself, kept the yard neat. Sometimes even after he's literally buried a body in the yard. Serial killers often have families and homes and are gainfully employed."

She steeples her hands, matching fingertip to fingertip. "Dennis Rader, known as BTK, who killed at least ten victims in Kansas, was married with two children, served honorably in the US Air Force, worked as a local government official, and was president of his church. Gary Ridgway, the Green River Killer, murdered at least forty-nine women. He worked at a truck factory and read the Bible on his breaks. His coworkers said he was quiet and had a nice smile." Her own face is unsmiling.

TESSA

Secret

"LET'S LOOK AT ARS'S FAMILY TREE," EL SAID. THEY were stretched out on the bed, hip to hip, so they could both look at the screen.

Did her tree have a blank space just waiting for Tessa's name?

But when El clicked, the tree had only eight people. The first was ARS herself. Then her parents, with just first names: Karen and Daniel. Karen's parents were listed as Annie and Frederick, with no last names, although it did have the years they were born. Daniel's parents were Heather and Brian Reinhart. The eighth person was Brian's father, Alfred "Alfie" Reinhart.

Tessa thought out loud. "If ARS's grandpa is

Brian Reinhart, then his son would be Daniel Reinhart, which means the R in ARS might stand for Reinhart." Her breath caught. She looked at El. "Maybe that's my last name, too—Reinhart?"

"Let me look at something." After clicking on DNA Matches, El typed "Reinhart" into the search bar for names in shared matches' trees. They were only a half dozen results, sorted from highest to lowest. After ARS, the largest amount of matching DNA with someone whose tree had a Reinhart was only 18 cM, a tiny fraction of what Tessa shared with ARS. El turned to look at her. "Sorry, I think the rest of these matches are too small for you to be a Reinhart by birth."

Tessa's excitement deflated, but El had already started clicking and typing again.

"After I bought the test, I started reading about how to use it to find your relatives. The first step is to assign a color to your highest match. What color do you want?"

"Blue?"

El clicked. "Next we look at Shared Matches." She tapped another button, and a new list of names appeared. "So this is everyone in Ancestry's database who shares DNA with both you and ARS. We're going to color code them all blue because you and all the rest of these people descended from the same person or couple. It could be recent or it could be pretty far back."

El finished labeling them blue and clicked back to the list of all Tessa's DNA matches.

Tessa sucked in her breath. The first thirteen were blue. "Why so many from one family?"

El shrugged. "Maybe that family likes to take DNA tests. Maybe everybody on that side had big families, so there's a greater chance someone tested. All I know is, if we can figure out how these people relate to one another, we might be able to figure out how they relate to you."

"How will we do that?"

"By checking out their family trees. Hopefully, they'll have more names and dates than ARS does."

El opened a new tab for each person with a family tree and began clicking back and forth, humming under her breath. Everything was happening too fast for Tessa to follow, not just physically, but emotionally. Rather than asking El to slow down, she closed her eyes and tried to concentrate on her breathing.

After a gap of time that might have been ten

minutes or an hour, El announced, "I'm starting to figure it out."

Tessa opened her eyes. Anticipation crackled between them like static electricity.

El pointed to the screen. "Look at this one match. They descend from a Frederick Baker and Annie Harris. Frederick and Annie, just like ARS had." She clicked on a different tab. "And this other person is descended from a Frederick Baker and an Annie with no last name."

Hope flickered inside Tessa, like a tiny flame struggling to ignite.

El chose another tab. "And this tree shows Frederick Baker's father was Joseph Baker, and…" She clicked again. "And this person doesn't have anything about Frederick Baker, but they are descended from Joseph Baker, who was born about twenty-three years before Frederick." Another tab. "And this person's last name is Harris. Just like Annie. It seems to me like the only way you could match these people who have Baker or Harris is if you are descended from a Baker who married a Harris: Frederick and Annie. I think they were your grandparents or maybe your great-grandparents."

Tessa knew she should be filled with joy. Instead, doubt twisted in her gut like a piece of broken glass. "But we don't have a paper trail or anything. We've got no proof."

El tapped the underside of Tessa's wrist. "You do have proof. It's in your blood. In your DNA. And we can still show how all these people are connected to one another with things like marriage licenses, census data, and obituaries. What we don't have, and what we will probably never have, is a paper trail connecting them to you."

"My parents—my adoptive parents—said I was only a few hours old when I was found at the fire station. And that the police checked all local hospitals and none was missing a newborn." Tessa took a deep breath. "I was somebody's secret."

"Maybe not for much longer," El said. "I think we should message this ARS."

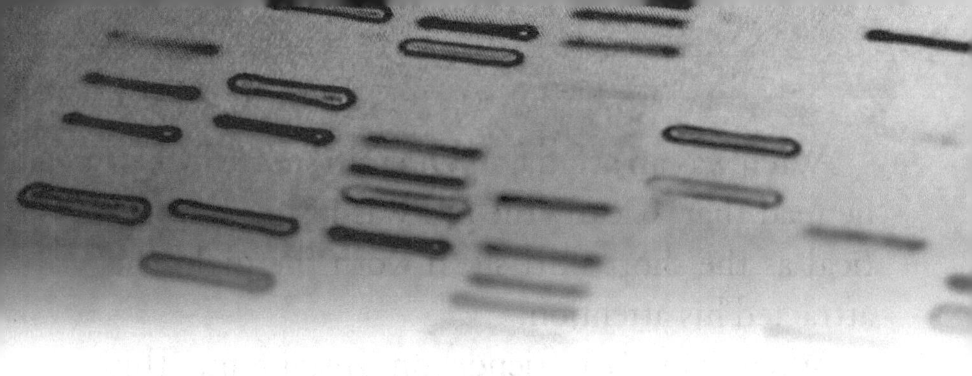

QUENTIN

Wrong

NINETEEN DAYS AFTER QUENTIN HAD LET THE GIRL he'd mentally dubbed Short Skirt go on her merry way, he found he couldn't stop thinking about her. Wren Phillips—the photo he had taken of her ID had revealed her true name— had become his little side project. But it was just practice, a way to keep his skills sharp.

Like many of the kids who danced at the club, Wren was a student at Bridgetown. Thanks to the many forms she had completed for school, he learned she was twenty-one and lived in an apartment complex populated mostly by other students. He learned her parents' names and the name of the small town where she'd grown up.

Wren was an art major. Quentin snorted when he read that. Clearly the girl was just as impractical as the short skirt she'd worn the night she attracted his attention.

Wren had 313 friends on Instagram. This now included one of the sock puppet accounts Quentin had set up years back. Back then, a few screen shots of an internet stranger were enough to start building an online personality. More recently, he had switched to AI-generated photos. He was fascinated by the possibilities of AI, how closely it mimicked reality, even on video. With AI, you could make a politician espouse views he had never held. You could create scenes that had never happened but looked like photographs. You could bring the dead back to life, at least virtually.

Quentin liked to scroll through Wren's Instagram posts. From photos, he figured out who her friends were: mostly girls who dressed in the same tarty way she did. Wren's regular clothes turned out not to be much better than her going-out clothes. They were all versions of the same formula: too short, too tight, showing too much skin. She reminded him of that marathoner, the one who had practically taunted Quentin every day by running through campus dressed in a running bra and skintight briefs more revealing than Melanie's actual underwear. Women like that were always flaunting themselves but quick to take offense if someone pointed it out.

The other constant on Wren's Instagram was a large spiral silver pin she wore on every jacket, every sweater, just as she had the night he walked her to her car. In one posting, he learned she had made it.

From how much they commented on each other's posts and showed up in each other's photos, he deduced she had a boyfriend. A boyfriend who didn't care enough to make sure his girlfriend kept herself covered up.

She was a walking temptation, an affront to decency. Wren Phillips needed discipline—just like the other girls he'd dealt with.

The only thing Quentin liked about Wren was she was predictable. She went to the same coffee shop each morning, walked the same route to and from her apartment, always studied at the same library table. On Saturdays, she liked to unwind at the same club where Quentin had first met her, dancing in ways that left little to the imagination.

Her predictability would make things so much easier. Not that he was going to do anything. It was too soon. But he liked to think about it.

Wren was the kind of girl who strutted around in short skirts, mocked her mother's concerns, and partied late into the night, without any regard for men like him. It was as if she were asking for something ugly to happen.

After checking out her latest post featuring a selfie in an off-the-shoulder blouse, Quentin logged out of Instagram and flicked off the lamp on his desk. As he sat in the darkness of his locked office, he couldn't help but imagine her fear if she ever understood who he really was. Her brown eyes would widen in shock and her porcelain skin would pale even further. He could almost taste the sweet terror that would fill the air around them.

"A little bird told me you didn't think you needed to worry about the Phantom," he would whisper.

And then he would show her how wrong she was.

TESSA

Chat

AFRAID SHE WOULD ACCIDENTALLY HIT THE SEND key before she was satisfied with her message to ARS, Tessa drafted it in a different program, then handed her laptop to El.

El read out loud. "Hey, it looks like we are related. My name is Tessa. I was born eighteen years ago and adopted into a wonderful home."

"Wonderful home" was what Tessa figured someone would want to hear. Not the reality that these days her parents were pretty checked out. That they barely noticed her, except when they snapped at her. Early yesterday morning, she had caught her dad hastily pulling a pillow and blanket from the couch.

El pursed her lips. "I've heard if you say you're adopted right up front, people get scared. They either know the truth and want to keep it covered up or they're afraid of finding out something they don't really want to know. You need to bring them on board gradually."

They went back and forth until they were both satisfied. Tessa copied and pasted the revised message into the program.

"Hi, I'm new to Ancestry and see we match at 480 cM. You are my highest match. I'm trying to figure out how we connect. Would love to chat." *Chat*, they had decided, sounded like a word an adult with a casual interest in genealogy would use.

Tessa took a deep breath and pressed the Send key.

Forty-five minutes later, just after El left, Tessa got a message notification from Ancestry. It was from ARS. Her fingers trembled as she clicked.

"I'm curious," the woman had written. "We don't have any Lundgrens in our family that I know of." She signed it "Audrey."

Tessa was too revved up to wait to run things past El. She typed, "I'm still trying to figure out things myself. I'm pretty sure I descend from Frederick Baker and Annie Harris. I match several people who descended from them, including you, and you are my closest match."

This time she had to wait only a few seconds for a reply.

"Have you asked your parents? Sometimes a generation back knows more."

Tessa hesitated. How long could she keep hiding the fact she was adopted? She settled for "Unfortunately, that's not possible." Maybe Audrey would think they were estranged or dead. The thought gave her a twinge. "Where do you live? I'm in Southwest Portland." After a second, she added, "Oregon."

"I'm in Tigard."

Tigard was only a few miles away. More proof they were related.

"Maybe we could get together for coffee and try to figure things out?" Tessa asked.

They made arrangements to meet at a Starbucks near Audrey at 10 AM on Saturday. When she told Victor, he asked if he could come, too.

Tessa bit her lip. "I don't want Audrey to feel outnumbered."

"We're in high school and she's an adult. And you need me. El's good at family trees, but I'm good at DNA math." He grinned at her. "Plus, I have a car and can drive us all there."

On Saturday, Victor picked up both El and Tessa at El's house. They arrived at Starbucks thirty minutes early and sat at a table for four. As they waited, Tessa examined the face of every incoming female patron. But then a woman walked through the door and she knew. Dark hair pulled back into a messy bun. Dark eyes. Pale skin. Her lips weren't as full as Tessa's and her face was more oval than heart-shaped, but she had the same sharply arched brows.

Tessa raised her hand and waved. "Audrey?"

At the sight of Tessa, Audrey's eyes widened. In a few quick strides, she reached the table.

Tessa stood. She didn't know what to do with her hands. It seemed weird to shake hands, so she held them dangling in front of her.

"This is quite the posse," Audrey said, but she didn't look put out.

"These are my friends El and Victor. They're helping me figure things out."

Audrey was still assessing Tessa. "I have to admit you're a lot younger than I thought. Do you mind if I ask how old you are?"

"Eighteen. We all go to the same school."

"High school seems like a long time ago now. I'm forty-three and a sous chef at Café de Lumière." She used what Tessa guessed was the correct French pronunciation. Her black sneakers, dark jeans, and abstract black-and-white short-sleeved top made her look younger.

"My parents took me there once," El said. "It was really good."

"Thanks," Audrey said in a distracted tone. "Let me just get an iced coffee." She looked down at the table. "Do you guys want anything else, like a pastry or something?"

"That's okay," Tessa said, while El and Victor shook their heads. Tessa hadn't been able to take more than a sip of her latte. While they sat silently and waited for Audrey to come back, Tessa clasped her trembling hands together, but it didn't help. Victor gave her a sympathetic look.

When Audrey returned, she said, "I just took

the test because there were rumors that we were part Cherokee. But zip." She sliced her free hand through the air. "After that, I kind of lost interest." She peered at Tessa again. "Maybe it's just a coincidence we have some DNA in common. Have you talked to any other relatives?"

Tessa chewed her lip. "I'm actually adopted. I was left at a fire station as a newborn."

Audrey's mouth opened, then closed.

Victor filled in the silence. "Four hundred eighty centimorgans is actually a lot. Mathematically, the most likely scenario is you and Tessa are first cousins, once removed."

Audrey's brows drew together. "What does removed mean exactly?"

El spoke up. "A first cousin is just what we mean when we say cousin. A first cousin once removed is your cousin's kid. The removed means it's a different generation."

Her dark brows drew together. "So you're saying one of my cousins had a kid I didn't know about, and that kid is Tessa?"

"That's what it looks like," Victor said.

Audrey fiddled with her straw. "You're only a year younger than my daughter. But as far as I know, no one in my family had a kid anywhere near the time you were born."

"Can I show you how I figured out you're related?" El asked, pointing to Tessa's laptop. When Audrey nodded, they scooted their chairs together and put their faces close to the screen. Victor and Tessa glanced at each other and then away.

El started by talking about Frederick Baker and Annie Harris, showing how many matches Tessa had with their descendants and other relatives. "Since Tessa's got matches on both the Baker and the Harris sides, she must be descended from one of their kids. They had four, right?"

Audrey frowned. "Yeah, but that's where everything starts narrowing down. Like, you have Fred Jr. in this tree, but he's dead. He died when he was twelve, maybe ten years before I was born. He was riding a bike, and back then nobody wore helmets."

Tessa winced.

Audrey tapped at another spot on the screen. "And there's my Uncle Doug. He only got married a few years ago." She paused. "To a very nice man."

"So he never dated women?" El asked. "Not even once?"

"I heard that even in high school he was out. So I don't think he had a secret child who then went on to have another secret child." Her eyes went wide. "What about my family? Could my brother have fathered a kid he doesn't know about?"

"No," Victor said definitively. "The amount of shared DNA for an uncle or aunt match would be about three times higher."

Audrey bit her thumbnail as she thought. "That just leaves my cousin Gina, my Aunt Patty's only kid. She's twelve years older than me. I used to think she was glamorous. When I was nine, she married this guy named Matthew McCoy. I had daydreamed about being a flower girl, walking down the aisle in a pretty dress. But he was a member of this weird church called the Reapers of Divine Judgment. Some people say it's a cult. They're strict about women and their place. And the ceremony was only open to other church members."

"A cult? You mean like those polygamists in Arizona?" Tessa asked. "El and I watched a documentary about them."

"No, not that bad." Audrey reconsidered. "Although still pretty bad. Like, they believe the man is in charge of everything. And they don't allow members to do a lot of normal things."

"Like what?" El asked.

"Like reading novels or watching TV, or celebrating birthdays or Christmas. Or women wearing pants or cutting their hair. That's all considered worldly. Matthew even cut off one of their kids for daring to go to college. If anyone from the church, or even his own family, runs into Jared, they're supposed to pretend they don't even see him."

Victor made a face.

"And Gina had to start dressing 'modestly'"—Audrey made air quotes—"shapeless dresses all the way to the ground, never showing her elbows or collarbone, always a little scarf on top of her head. And she started having kids right away. There were seven in all. I guess with you, eight. They don't believe in birth control, of course. For a while, her husband let the kids go to a regular school, but then when I was in college, they switched to homeschooling. Every year, I send Gina and her kids Christmas cards just to remind her the real world still exists. I feel bad for her kids growing up in that crazy church."

"The number of centimorgans fits." Victor turned to Tessa. "Gina must be your mom."

"But if she had all those kids, why would she give one up?" Tessa asked.

Audrey answered. "Maybe she realized how toxic that church is for girls. Good for Gina. She must still have had a little spark in her."

Tessa frowned. "Wouldn't someone have noticed she was pregnant?"

Audrey put her hand on her own flat stomach. "The dresses they wear are more like sacks. You could be nine months pregnant and no one would know." She picked up her phone and started scrolling. "She doesn't have a phone number or an email address, of course. But I do have her physical address."

"They don't believe in email?" El snorted. "Or phones?"

"Again, 'worldly.'" Audrey stopped scrolling. "If you go visit, I would do it during the weekday, when her husband is at work. From what I've seen of him, he's an angry man who exerts complete control over his family. If he finds out what Gina did, well…" She let her words trail off.

Something inside Tessa went still. She had imagined her father in many different ways.

But never as dangerous.

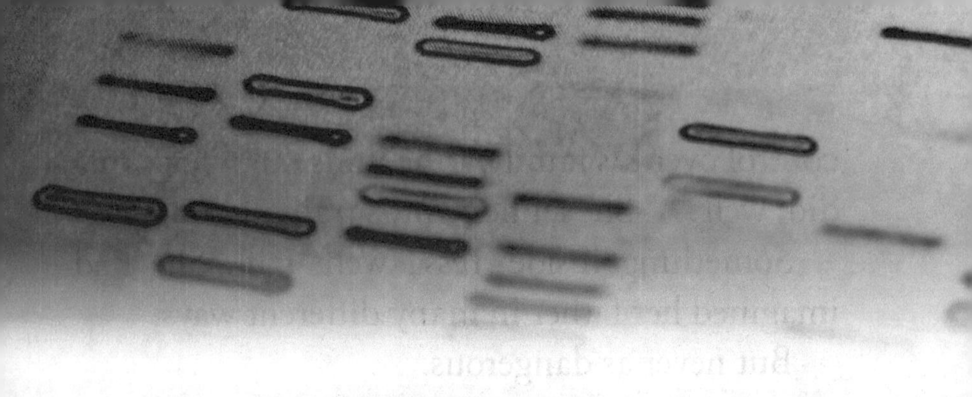

QUENTIN

Rules

ALIDA HAD BEEN A FRESHMAN WHEN SHE FIRST caught Quentin's eye. He hadn't yet been named head of security, so he still worked the occasional late shift. One evening he had discovered her tucked in a shadowy corner of the parking garage, making out with a boy. Quentin had shone the beam of his silver flashlight (big enough to double as a weapon, if need be) up her long legs and then across her face. Even with her eyes closed, it was strong enough to make her wince.

He had demanded their IDs and then handed them back while instructing them to return to their dorms. Alida had started to protest, but the boy had enough sense to grab her hand and pull her away.

Two months later, he had found Alida in the same spot. Only this time the person passionately embracing her had been another girl.

And when he asked for IDs, Alida had defiantly held his gaze, a spark of rebellion in her eyes. "You can't arrest us for loving each other," she'd said, putting her hand on the small of the other girl's back. Looking terrified, the girl had twisted away from Alida's touch.

He hadn't arrested them, of course. He was a campus cop with limited powers and no mandate to enforce morality. "Go home," Quentin had said, his voice taking on a dangerous edge. "Both of you."

But Alida stuck in his mind, the image of those two girls together stirring something deep within him. After that, his gaze lingered on her whenever he saw her on campus.

And he made a point of seeing her. Alida had become a project, one Quentin continued even after she graduated, got a job, moved into a little run-down rental. He learned where she worked, her favorite café, the park where she ran in the early morning. He figured out her roommate, Odessa, was more than just someone to split the rent with, but that she was also not Alida's only partner.

A secret spectator, he watched Alida's life unfold from a distance. She acted as if there were no rules.

But there were rules, and eventually Quentin explained them to her.

TESSA

Doubt

AFTER MEETING WITH AUDREY, THE THREE OF them walked out to Victor's car. As they buckled their seat belts, El said, "So when are we going to pay your mom a visit?"

At the words *your mom*, Tessa felt a buzzing in her veins. "Audrey said the best time was weekdays, but what about school?" Thinking of actually coming face-to-face with her mother was like inching toward the edge of a cliff.

Victor shrugged. "Yeah, but we're allowed to leave campus during lunch. With luck, we could be back in time for biology."

Doubt itched like a scab. What if this was all just a series of bad guesses? What if Gina wasn't really her mom? Would that be such a bad thing? Of all the moms and dads she and El had fantasized about, religious fanatics hadn't crossed their minds.

El squeezed her shoulder. "Let's do it."

Tessa took a deep breath. "Okay. Monday." She would rip off the scab and see what was underneath.

After Victor dropped El off at her house, he turned to Tessa. "What's your address?"

"I live on Terrace Heights, but would you mind letting me out a block earlier?"

He looked away, pinching his silver earring in the shape of a lightning bolt.

She hurried to explain. "If my parents see your car, they might ask what we were doing. And I don't want to tell them anything until I actually have answers."

He did as she asked. As he pulled over, Tessa turned to face him. She was suddenly aware of his straight nose, the thick fringe of his eyelashes, the bow of his mouth.

He didn't say anything, just looked from her eyes to her lips and back again. Was he getting ready to kiss her? Did she want him to kiss her?

Or would that just muddy the waters of their friendship?

In a panic, Tessa reached behind her and found the door handle. Calling, "See you Monday!" she scrambled out.

She watched him drive away. Wondering where Victor lived made Tessa think about maps, and that made her realize she had overlooked one piece of information that might confirm their theory.

When she walked into her house, she found her mom unloading groceries in the kitchen.

"Mom, where was the fire station I was found at?"

Her mom stilled, a can of low-sodium tomato soup in each hand. "Why do you want to know?"

"Just curious." From the reusable bags on the floor, Tessa picked up a box of Wheat Thins and another of soda crackers and put them on the shelf, careful not to look directly at her mom. Normally, Tessa couldn't hide anything from her, but these days her parents were so lost in their thoughts she felt like a ghost around them.

"It was off Highway 26, about twenty minutes from here."

"Thanks." Opening the refrigerator door, she puzzle-pieced the various permutations of milk the family drank to make room for the new cartons.

"Did you want to go visit it or something?"

"No, like I said, I was just curious." Tessa stacked oranges in the blue bowl on the counter. Finally, all the groceries were put away, and she could escape to her room. From Audrey's message, she copied Gina's address. Then she pasted it into Google Maps and looked for the nearest fire station.

A cold finger traced Tessa's spine. Gina's home was less than half a mile from where she had been found.

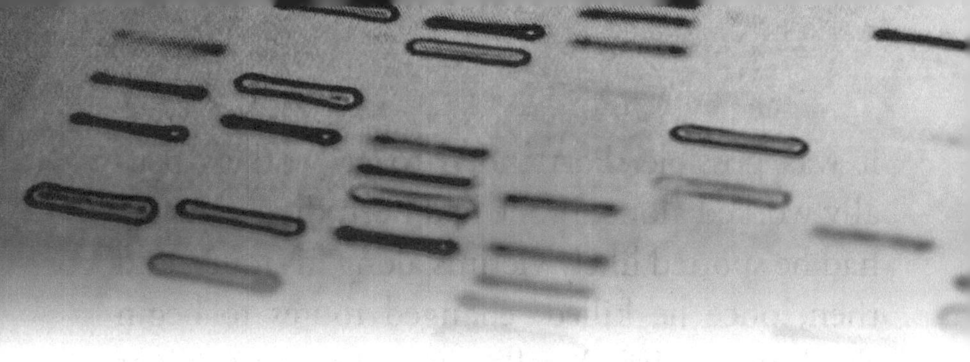

KEISHA

Confident

KEISHA HAD SPENT MOST OF THE DAY REVIEWING information from the tip line. It had started up after Kylie Williams's murder, so some tips went back years. Callers were sure the Phantom was their neighbor, their son-in-law, their coworker. They recalled peculiar incidents, strange conversations, and oddly timed absences. One woman even claimed her ex-husband must be the Phantom because he'd always had a fascination with crime shows.

It was overwhelming, and 99 percent of it was garbage.

In fact, more than one caller had been sure it was their actual garbage man. Keisha guessed it was possible. Portland garbage workers usually worked alone. If one had been the Phantom, had he spotted likely victims along his route, and then, once he killed, changed routes to begin the hunt again? A reflective safety vest might even have disarmed a young woman answering a door.

If the Phantom was like most serial killers, the crime would begin as a fantasy, building until he was ready to act on it. But the reality would never be as good as he had imagined. After a cooling-off period, the cycle would start over. But even as the pressure to kill again grew, the Phantom always maintained enough caution to attack a solitary female, someone with no known connection to him.

Was it really true that the Phantom and Alida or any of the other victims had been strangers? To the victim, yes, he might have been unknown until their fatal meeting. But in order to succeed time after time, the victim had probably not been a stranger to the Phantom. He must have gotten to know each one: where they lived, who they lived with, where they worked, when they exercised, what their daily routine was. That would have been part of the process. Part of the buildup. Watching, thinking, planning.

What made it even more horrific was his success at remaining unknown and unknowable. Nothing defined him more than his elusiveness. He truly was a phantom. After sixteen years of successfully eluding capture, he now must be incredibly confident.

Which made him even more dangerous.

# TESSA

Outsiders

AFTER TEXTING VICTOR AND EL ABOUT HOW CLOSE the fire station was to Gina's house, Tessa logged in to Ancestry. She found the section of scanned yearbooks. Audrey had told them Gina's maiden name—Ewing—as well as the name of her high school. After finding the right year, Tessa scanned through the virtual pages until she came to the *E*'s. And there she was. Gina Ewing. The woman who was probably her mom.

Tessa leaned closer. Gina's smile looked uncertain. The right side of her lipsticked mouth rose a little higher than the left. Tessa had seen that same crooked smile in her own photos. And the high cheekbones looked like hers. But Gina's face was rounder than Tessa's. Even though the photo must have been taken when she was about Tessa's age, Gina looked younger, unfinished.

Her long, straight hair fell past her shoulders. Tessa's hair wasn't straight, but she didn't think Gina's was really either. Her hair rose above the top of her head like it had been teased, and her bangs were spider-leg wispy. The style looked like it was trying too hard.

Tessa couldn't find any photos of Gina's husband, Matthew McCoy. The man who was probably her biological father. How creepy was it that he had been thirteen years older than Gina? That he made her join his weird church? Audrey had said they had married less than a year after Gina graduated from high school. Maybe it had been a relief to give up makeup and hair care and trying to figure out who she wanted to be.

All weekend, Tessa prepared. She put a half dozen of her baby pictures in her purse, as well as the cigar box holding the nightgown she'd been found in. At Target, she bought a long black dress with an empire waist. It not only was modest, but it also drew attention to her face. She imagined Gina's eyes widening when she saw Tessa. She would immediately know who she really was.

On Monday, she ate breakfast in her pajamas so no one would ask why she was wearing such a nice dress to school. But looking at her parents' shadowed faces, Tessa realized she could have dressed like a circus clown and they wouldn't have noticed. Her dad, in particular, looked as if he had aged years in the past few weeks. His shirt hung off his bony shoulders, and his breakfast appeared untouched. How long would it be before her parents admitted they were breaking up?

At lunch, when Tessa walked out to the parking lot, Victor was already there, leaning against his old green Honda. Their only shared class was biology, so he hadn't yet seen her.

He tilted his head. "You dressed up."

Tessa's face warmed. "I just don't want to offend Gina."

El walked up in jeans and a T-shirt. Her colorful hair was mostly hidden by a baseball cap.

On the fifteen-minute drive, the three were quiet as Victor's music streamed through the speakers.

Occasionally, Google Maps would interrupt the Spanish words to tell him when to turn.

Tessa followed the route on her phone. She pointed. "That's the firehouse where I was left."

Victor parked a few houses away from the McCoys'. He turned off the car's engine, but no one moved. Then Tessa wiped her damp palms on her dress, took a deep breath, and got out. The McCoys lived in a blue ranch-style house. Framed by the living room window were two chairs and a faded blue couch. They faced, not a TV, but a broad brick fireplace. On the mantelpiece was what appeared to be a well-thumbed Bible. A woman sat in one of the chairs. Underneath a black scarf, her long salt-and-pepper hair was pulled back into a fishtail braid.

Tessa's blood thrummed in her ears. Was this her mother, at long last?

She climbed the stairs to the porch. El and Victor were on either side of her and a step back. Nailed to the wall was a gold-and-black sign. NO SOLICITORS. She took a deep breath and knocked.

She watched the woman turn toward the door. Tessa still couldn't see her face. Then slowly, deliberately, she turned back.

Tessa knocked longer and harder. She would knock as long as she had to.

Finally, the woman pushed herself up and came to the door. She opened it only a crack.

"Didn't you see the sign?" Her voice was low, like Tessa's. "No solicitors." She started to close the door.

"Gina?" Tessa asked urgently. "Your cousin Audrey gave me your address."

The older woman didn't open the door any wider, but she didn't keep closing it either. "Didn't she tell you we don't talk to outsiders?"

"I just have"—Tessa had to stop and swallow—"a question about something that happened almost exactly eighteen years ago."

The woman suddenly poked her head and shoulders past the doorframe. Startled, Tessa stepped back, right onto Victor's foot. He steadied her elbow with his hand.

Gina—because it had to be Gina, who else could it be?—scanned the street. Then she opened the door and said, "Come in. Hurry."

Tessa reminded herself to breathe. Her eyes never left Gina's face.

The other woman was supposedly fifty-five,

but she looked far older, with deep wrinkles and hair more silver than black. The uncertain, slightly plump girl from the yearbook had hardened into a weathered, brittle woman with a challenging gaze. She was half a head shorter than Tessa. Her voluminous black dress hung loose around her thin frame. Eighteen years ago, it wouldn't have been hard to conceal a full-term pregnancy underneath it.

Tessa had done some reading about their church with the weird name. In their view, nearly everything was "worldly." Maybe that included sunscreen. Or dental care. Because Gina's mouth looked sunken, as if she were missing teeth. But Tessa could still see the similarities in the shapes of their features. Would this be what she would look like when she was old?

"Where did you park?" Gina demanded, her hands twisting together.

"Down the block," Victor said.

"So, September third, eighteen years ago?" Tessa insisted. "Does that date mean anything?"

Gina's lips pressed together to make a white line. But now her dark eyes looked pleading, almost desperate. "Where is she?"

"I'm right here." Tessa tapped her chest. "I'm your daughter." She searched Gina for echoes of herself, how she moved her hands, the length of her fingers, even the shape of her fingernails. She saw similarities, but also differences. Would the same be true of any random woman?

Gina's mouth fell open, revealing two dark gaps. "What are you talking about? Where's Ruth? Where's my daughter?"

Ruth must be the name she had given Tessa in her head. "Just after I was born September third, eighteen years ago, I was left at a fire station. I was adopted into a happy family. But I just had my DNA tested. My closest connection was your cousin Audrey. We match at four hundred eighty centimorgans. That means I'm one of Audrey's cousin's children. And after I talked to her, I know the only cousin it can be is—you."

Gina's face looked like she tasted something bitter. "And you think I would do that to a child of mine? Abandon them in the godless world?" She snorted. "You're not my daughter!"

"Then why," El asked, "did your face change when you heard what day Tessa was born?"

"September third is the day my daughter Ruth ran away. It was a mistake allowing her to go to public school." She spat the words at them. "They taught her to be worldly, to be immodest, to dis- respect her elders." It was clear Gina thought the same of Tessa, El, and Victor. "After she left, I started homeschooling all my children, the way I should have from the beginning. Ruth chose to leave her family, her church, and her God. She chose to damn her soul."

Victor had begun rapidly typing into his phone. "Or maybe she did something else. At four hundred eighty centimorgans, there's an eighty-nine percent chance Tessa and Audrey are first cousins once removed or half first cous- ins. But there's also a seven percent chance you and Audrey are first cousins, twice removed. Two generations different, not just one." His eyes found Tessa's. "It just made sense Gina was your mother. But if this Ruth ran away the day you were born, I'm thinking *she* must be your mother. Ruth must have given birth to you and then taken you to the fire station before getting on a bus or something."

Gina made a scoffing noise. "How dare you! Ruth was only a child! An innocent. She couldn't have been pregnant. She was only fifteen."

But Tessa saw it in the older woman's eyes. That she believed.

That Gina knew Tessa was her granddaughter.

Maxwell Holloway and psychologist Dr. Evelyn Thornfield sit in matching armchairs. He leans forward.

"So why do sometimes two or three years go between killings? Does that mean there are more bodies out there we haven't found?" His voice thrums when he says "more bodies."

Dr. Thornfield shakes her head. "While the killer's calling cards are disturbing, they also mean we know there are no missing bodies out there. Otherwise, we would have items we couldn't associate with a previous victim. And the killer clearly wants to be credited with every kill." Her lips are a slash of scarlet. "A gap can be caused by many things. The BTK Killer, Dennis Rader, seemed to take breaks when he had young children.

Sometimes a break means the perpetrator is in prison. Or they've moved or traveled out of the area. Or maybe they had a close brush with getting caught. Or they may have found a substitute that partially addresses their urges. Rader got a job as a compliance officer, which meant he got to exercise a degree of control over the general public. And controlling others is what these serial killers are all about."

She speaks directly to the camera. "But I personally believe the aftermath of the killing is just as important to him. He enjoys the fear percolating within the community. I believe the Phantom is driven not just by the act of extinguishing lives but also by orchestrating fear."

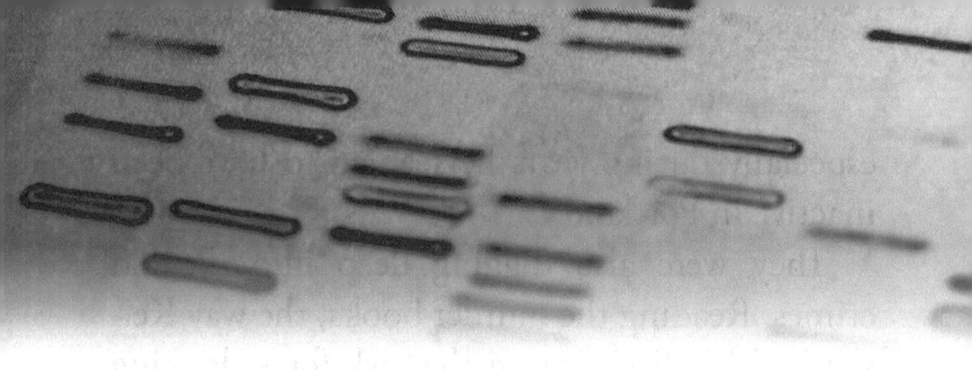

KEISHA

Gaps

WITH SHANE'S BLESSING, KEISHA TOUCHED BASE with Mrs. Cleary by phone nearly every day. She couldn't share specifics, not that there were many specifics to share. But it was important to make Mrs. Cleary feel like she hadn't been forgotten. That her daughter hadn't been forgotten. To make her feel like she didn't need to hit the streets again with a megaphone and a poster.

While the bulk of the investigation was still centered on Alida, the focus had also broadened. Members of the task force were creating timelines to look for patterns and gaps. They checked with neighboring states again to see if they had any unsolved crimes fitting the Phantom's MO, especially during years he seemed to have been inactive in Portland.

They were also digging deep into the old crimes. Reading the murder books, the way Keisha had her first day on the task force, looking for the smallest overlooked clue. Reinterviewing witnesses, family members, and associates of the victims. Sometimes the passage of time could lead to new information, as relationships changed or even fractured. A divorce or a death could change what people might be willing to say about a husband or brother.

Shane kept the pressure on the Phantom by telling the media every day they were making progress. The hope was to make him sweat a little. Shane was also careful to never call the Phantom a madman or a maniac. No need to needle him into doing something even worse.

"At some point, all serial killers make a mistake," Shane said at the end of today's morning meeting of the task force. "You just never know what that mistake's going to be."

TESSA

Roots

GINA HAD INSISTED THEY NEEDED TO LEAVE—immediately. The drive back to school was a blur. While El and Victor animatedly discussed what had happened, Tessa tried to accept that her real mother was nothing like any of the versions she and El had imagined. Not rich or famous or beautiful. Not even a woman, but a girl.

After school, the three of them regrouped around Tessa's dining room table with a pack of Oreos (vegan, but only technically, in Tessa's opinion) and glasses of milk (oat for El).

Tessa sent a quick update to Audrey, and then they checked all the social media platforms. They found a few Ruth McCoys, but never one who was both white and remotely the right age.

"Maybe she got married and changed her name." Tessa pinched the bridge of her nose.

As she spoke, a reply from Audrey popped up. "Fascinating! As far as I know, all of Ruth's brothers and sisters are still in the church except for Jared. He's the next oldest, just a year younger than Ruth. He might be in touch with her." It included his address.

In contrast to his sister, Jared seemed to be on every social media platform. His content was heavy on pictures—mostly his French bulldog or fancy-looking cocktails—and light on specifics. He never took selfies.

"Let's make another field trip tomorrow," El suggested. "Only after dinner in case Jared's got a day job." When Victor said it was his little sister's birthday, they agreed to go in two days.

At dinner that night, Tessa said, "I'm going to do my homework at El's." The lie came easily. Who was she becoming? Was she making a mistake?

Instead of reminding Tessa of what time she needed to be home, the way he normally would, her dad just pushed his untouched plate away.

It was a chicken-and-broccoli pasta dish he normally loved. He got to his feet.

"Lars." Her mom's voice had an edge. "You have to eat. You're nothing but skin and bones."

His jaw tightened. "I keep telling you, I'm not hungry." He left the room.

As she waited down the street for Victor to pick her up, Tessa's mind couldn't settle. While she was busy searching for her biological family, was she losing her own? Would her parents fight over custody? The house?

Jared lived in Northwest Portland in a new-looking, four-story apartment building. They got lucky, arriving just as someone else was leaving so they could enter the lobby. When they located his apartment on the second floor, Tessa rang the bell.

Jared opened the door just wide enough to stick his head out. Tessa took a step back. They each had a slight gap between their front teeth and the same high cheekbones.

An all-black French bulldog squirmed between Jared's legs. Barking and growling, he stood on his hind legs, as if challenging anyone who might believe he was not much bigger than a cat. His barks sounded more like sneezes.

"Rocket!" Jared admonished, grabbing his leather collar.

"OMG, he's so cute!" El crouched before the dog, offering her closed hand.

"Can I help you?" Jared brought his eyes back to Tessa.

"Are you Jared McCoy?" When he nodded, she said, "I'm Tessa Lundgren, and these are my friends El and Victor. Your cousin Audrey gave us your address."

"Why'd she do that?" His mouth tensed.

"We've been doing genealogical research and hit a roadblock. We tried to talk to your mom, but since we're not members of her church…" Tessa let her voice trail off.

Jared snorted. "It's not a church. It's a bunch of deluded people who pretend to believe in a made-up God so they can dictate other people's lives. They don't even allow pets, because they're supposedly a tool of Satan to distract from God." He scooped up Rocket.

"I take it you're not a fan," Tessa said.

Jared looked at her a long moment before saying, "Why don't you come in?" He put Rocket down inside the spotless apartment. A guy in his early thirties was watching a true crime TV show, but when he saw them, he turned it off.

"This is my boyfriend, Harvey." Jared settled down on the love seat next to him.

After introducing themselves to Harvey, they sat on the couch, with Tessa in the middle.

"So what kind of genealogical research are you doing?" Jared asked.

"We just wanted to ask you some questions about your older sister," Tessa said. "About Ruth."

His expression changed. "What did you want to know? And why?"

"When was the last time you heard from her?"

"A little over eighteen years ago." He leaned forward. "Do you know where she is?"

Tessa's eyes burned. "I've never met her."

"Then why are you asking about her?"

"Because," she started, and couldn't complete the sentence. "Because…"

Victor laid his hand on hers. "Because Tessa was adopted as a newborn eighteen years ago. Her closest match on Ancestry is your cousin Audrey. We believe Tessa's mother might be your sister. Might be Ruth."

Jared made a surprised sound. "That's not

possible." He turned to Harvey. "You've heard me talk about Ruth. The brave one. She made it possible for me to leave. But there was no way she was pregnant. She was only fifteen when she left."

"You don't need to be an adult to get pregnant," El pointed out. "Isn't that exactly the kind of person who would get pregnant at fourteen and hide it?"

Jared snorted. "If she did—and I'm not saying I believe you—it would be on her. According to the Reapers, it's a woman's job to keep men's lust in check. They have to wear shapeless dresses and headscarves, and never makeup, pants, shorts, or even short sleeves. Men can't wear white or tan pants, or white shoes. I'm not sure of the reasoning behind those last three."

"Crimes of fashion," El said.

Jared's lips lifted briefly. "We didn't have any mirrors at home because we were supposed to reflect on our relationship with God. Women can't cut their hair or dye it. Men can't have hair past their ears. Nobody can have piercings or tattoos." He traced the tropical flowers on his arm.

El leaned forward. "You could hide a lot underneath that dress your mom was wearing."

"But we were always together as a family. We worshipped every morning and went to church Wednesday nights, Saturday mornings, and all day Sundays. There was no time or place for my sister to get pregnant."

"What about at school?" Tessa asked.

He pinched his lips together. "The other kids made fun of her. They didn't understand it wasn't her choice to dress like she belonged behind a butter churn or to have hair so long she could sit on it."

After unzipping her backpack, Tessa pulled the handmade pink nightgown from the cigar box.

Jared's eyes widened. He reached for it. "Where did you get that?"

Tessa resisted the urge to pull it back. "I was found wrapped in this at the fire station near your house."

"Oh my God. This was hers." He lifted the fabric to hide his face.

Harvey patted his shoulder while Tessa and her friends looked at one another awkwardly. Finally, Jared pulled the nightgown away.

"I don't know how it happened, but I believe you. You're Ruth's daughter. I think that's why

I let you in. Because you look like her. She was petite, and you're taller, but your face, the way you move your hands…" His voice trailed off. "Your voice even sounds like hers."

A mingled sorrow and joy washed over Tessa. If only she could see her, see the resemblance for herself. "So you don't have any idea where Ruth is?"

"I've looked online. I've asked other people who've left the church. But no one knows anything. Maybe she changed her name. It would be safer. People who leave—sometimes the church forces them to come back."

"Do you have *any* guesses about who my father could have been?"

Jared blew air through pursed lips. "You weren't permitted to be alone with a member of the opposite sex. That's called an 'occasion for sin.' They never thought about me being with another boy." He patted Harvey's knee. "When Ruth ran away, she was just starting sophomore year, so she must have gotten pregnant in January or February. And it must have happened at school. I guess it could have been any of the boys there."

Harvey spoke up. "If you used DNA to figure out Jared's sister was your mom, can't you do the same thing for your dad?"

"All of Tessa's paternal matches are pretty distant," Victor said, "and there aren't that many."

"You said you used Ancestry," Harvey said. "What about the other services? I've heard you should fish in all the ponds."

"What does that mean?" El asked.

"Most people just put their DNA on one site. Some of the others, like GEDmatch, let you upload your Ancestry results for free. You might find a match that way."

El put Tessa's anxiety into words. "Maybe the father was an adult. Like a teacher or a church leader?"

Jared's mouth twisted. "Whoever it was, she wouldn't have been allowed to keep you. They would've given you to an older couple to raise and Ruth would have been pruned back."

"Pruned back?" Victor echoed.

"They lock you in a room and no one is allowed to talk to you. That lasts until you repent." He pinched the bridge of his nose. "And that's actually considered the lighter punishment."

"What could be worse than that?" Tessa asked, imagining her mother's terror.

"Being uprooted. You're turned out of the church. Basically, it's like you're dead. If your friends or family pass you on the street, they're supposed to pretend they don't see or hear you. And meanwhile, you have no idea how to live in the real world. You've never used a cell phone or eaten at a restaurant."

"So you were uprooted," El said gently. It wasn't a question.

"I uprooted myself by going to college, which was worldly. I'd worn out my knees begging God to change me, to make me love women, but it didn't work. So I decided I might as well do everything I'd always wanted to."

"That's where we met," Harvey said. "I couldn't get over this guy at first. He didn't know how to work a remote or play a video game or order takeout."

Jared smiled at him. "I didn't even know how to cook, because that's women's work. I'd never stayed in a hotel or watched a movie. Do you know how many times in the real world people reference movie lines? I still don't get most of them. But you learn how to put your roots down in different soil." He straightened up and snapped his fingers.

"What is it?" Harvey asked.

"When my parents realized Ruth had taken off, they got rid of everything she hadn't taken with her. Gave her clothes to the other girls, and threw out the rest. But before they did, I took her journal. She must have forgotten to take it with her."

"Can I see it?" Tessa's voice shook.

Jared put his hand over Tessa's. "It's the only thing I have of hers, so I keep it in a safe-deposit box. But yes, I'll let you read it."

Maxwell Holloway leans toward the camera. "Now we turn to the fourth victim of the Portland Phantom. Bettina Martinez, known to her friends as Betty. Betty was just twenty-two when her life came to a tragic end at the very coffee shop where she worked. A place that once brewed warmth and community was now tainted by the shadows of unspeakable horror."

The camera cuts to a dramatic reenactment of the crime, showing the exterior of a small coffee shop, the only light in the darkness before dawn. A woman with two dark braids backs up against a silver cooler, her hands raised ineffectually while a hulking figure, his face hidden by a hoodie, stalks toward her.

Back on camera, Holloway raises an eyebrow. "At first glance, investigators believed this to be a simple robbery gone awry, a mistake we've seen before. But as they peeled back the layers, another narrative emerged. In Betty's apron pocket was something unexpected. A photograph, not of her own family or friends, but of Kylie's mother." His eyes gleam and his voice carries an unsettling delight. "Suddenly, these seemingly isolated tragedies intersected, and the intricate web woven by the Portland Phantom tightened. Betty had become yet another victim of the city's most notorious serial killer."

From Ruth's journal

August 21

My first journal! I feel so sophisticated! This afternoon my mom asked me to get her some eggs from the store. Of course I said yes. I love hearing the music overhead. It's so worldly, all these forbidden thoughts about love. Since I was by myself, I didn't have to keep my face blank. I even dared hum along when the chorus played a third time.

When I spotted this notebook with its black-and-white cover on the back-to-school sale table, I had to have it. I bought it with the eggs and threw away the receipt. Before I walked into our house, I slipped the notebook down my dress. All Reaper women know that's a good place to hide something. I hid it in my dresser drawer in the room I share with my sisters. This journal will be just for me. The one place where I can be myself, whoever that is, without anyone else judging.

And in three days I start high school!!

August 22

Most Reapers homeschool. But since my mom grew up in the world, she's always done a few things that raised eyebrows, like listening to recorded classical music or working as a bookkeeper for my dad's furniture business. When I was five, she suggested I start public kindergarten. Mom pointed out if she had to spend all her time teaching us, Dad would have to hire her replacement, and school is free. Since there were already a half dozen Reaper families

at Hillside K–8, he agreed. So I
went, and then Jared and Naomi
and Benjamin and the rest when
they were old enough. Now Mom
has pulled off her biggest move yet—
getting Dad's approval to let me
attend Brookwillow High. I'll be
the only one there from the church.

I had to swear I would eat lunch
alone and not break bread with
unbelievers. That I wouldn't even
glance at a novel or magazine
and that I would never, ever talk to
boys.

These are the same rules for
Hillside, but my dad says they're
extra important now I'm a woman.
A woman. I like the sound of that. At
the same time, I'm afraid he'll want
to betroth me soon, and marry me off
once I turn seventeen. So I'm going
to savor every minute.

August 24

Today was my first day of high school. I walked my brothers and sisters over to Hillside and then walked by myself to Brookwillow, which starts an hour later.

As soon as I turned the corner, I stuffed my headscarf into my backpack. Scripture says a woman who uncovers her head causes herself shame, but I know it's going to be hard enough to fit in.

By the time I arrived, sweat was trickling down my spine. I tried pushing up my sleeves, but that didn't make me any cooler, not with my dress brushing the ground and my neckline halfway up my throat. When the other students showed up, they were wearing shorts and tank tops. At Hillside, people were used to us, but Brookwillow has students from

all different middle schools, and most
have clearly never seen a Reaper
before. People stared at my clothes,
while I tried not to stare at all the
skin they exposed.

I saw a few people from Hillside,
and they nodded, but that was it. Is
this a mistake?

August 27

I wanted this so badly. I can't let
on how I feel lonely and lost. The
other kids talk about going to parties,
who's blowing up on social media,
who just got together or broke up.
They use a lot of slang or talk about
things I can't follow.

I remind myself that's not important to our souls. As the Bible says,
all that is of the world, the lust of the
flesh and the lust of the eyes and the
pride of life, is not of the Father but is
of the world.

But sometimes I can't help thinking I want to be of the world. I want to debate what color to paint my toenails, listen to music, discuss the latest movie, wear short dresses. I want to experience the world I've been warned against, the one that seems so colorful.

I want to be...normal.

But instead, I'm the silent observer, lurking on the fringes.

September 4

Philippians says we should only think about things that are true and pure and virtuous.

Nothing is honest or pure about adultery, violence, premarital sex, drug use. Yet these, according to my elders, are what novels and TV shows are all about. They say these false stories inflame lust, incite hatred, and dismiss God entirely, except to take his name in vain.

But Jesus was a storyteller. When he spoke about the prodigal son or the parable of the sower, it's clear he didn't mean a real-life person. Yet there was a deeper truth to his stories. Can't the same hold true now?

As eldest, it's my job to get the other children to sleep. The best way is by telling them a story. I start in the boys' room because they're the loudest, especially Jared. After they're asleep, I move on to the girls. Sometimes I tell stories from the Bible, like Daniel in the lions' den. Other times I make up my own, about brave children who face down snarling dogs or swim across treacherous rivers. And when I'm sure my parents won't overhear, the stories might be about defeating terrifying monsters or wicked witches. My siblings watch me with bright eyes, quiet for once, until one by one they drop off to sleep.

Tonight I told them about a girl who found a magical flower that illuminated her path whenever she got lost. As her journeys took her farther from home, the light of the flower grew more radiant.

Is it wrong to have magic in my stories? Those are the tales they want to hear again and again.

But am I sinning? The fear I will displease the Lord or, worse still, my parents is like a cold river running through me.

September 7

My mom wanted me to go to Brookwillow so I would know more than the other Reaper girls. They can read instructions and do basic math, but that's about it.

But when I'm not in class, I'm thinking about other things.

What would it be like to walk down the hall with a group of friends, giggling over shared secrets? To wear jeans that hug my legs? To feel a boy's calloused hand take mine?

But these are sinful thoughts, forbidden fantasies. I must cast them aside and focus on righteousness. The Bible says, "What does it profit a man if he gains the whole world, but loses his immortal soul?"

But some days a soul seems pretty small compared with the whole world.

September 9

Can I choose what I want to be? Am I a Reaper only because my parents are? My dad was born into it, my mom chose it (or at least chose my dad after he first sold her a dresser and then persuaded her to convert), but we kids didn't have any choice.

I'm sure my parents and the elders would say that kind of thinking is worldly.

But is it wrong?

September 15

As a Reaper, I've grown up without mirrors. But at school, every time I go into the bathroom, I see myself. I try not to look when anyone else is there, because then I see the other girls staring at my homemade clothes, my long hair, my bare face. But I can't help taking an occasional glimpse. Every single thing about me is different from the others.

Sometimes in class I say I have to visit the facilities. I lie, in other words. Gazing in the mirror, I fold up my long hair until it looks short. I hike up my dress and examine my legs.

What if people could see me in normal clothes, with normal hair?

Would boys think I was pretty?

September 17

If my dad knew what I was thinking, he would pull me out of here so fast my head would spin. I would be pruned back or even uprooted. How would I survive without my family, my community? If I were cast out in the darkness, I don't think I could survive.

September 23

I am writing this in the bathroom, when everyone is asleep. It's the only time I can be alone. And Naomi is such a little tattletale—she would love to spill all my secrets to our parents and maybe even to the elders.

I've met someone at school who takes me seriously. Who talks to me.

Who wants to know more about me.
But the more we talk, the more I
realize I have to be careful. Even with
what I write in this notebook.

October 1

I wish I could see him more often.
There are whole days I don't catch
more than a passing glimpse, and
I feel like a plant in need of water.
When he looks at me, suddenly I'm
not invisible anymore.

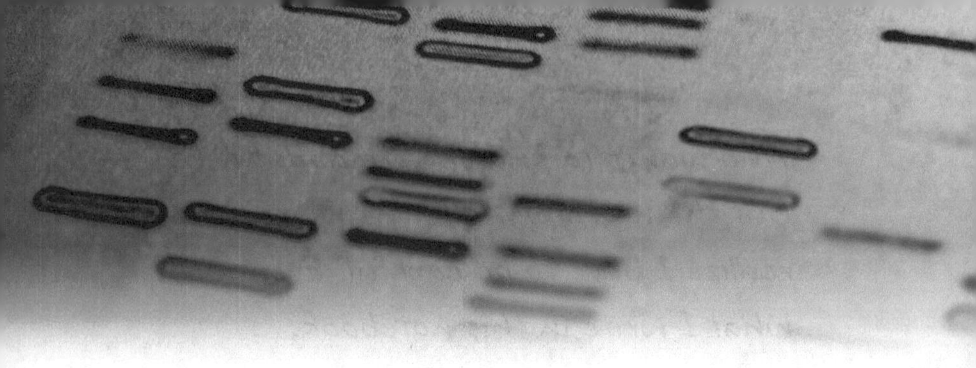

QUENTIN

Imagination

Nineteen years earlier

QUENTIN HAD BEEN A PATROL OFFICER FOR TWO years when the school resource officer at Brookwillow High School retired. He put his name in.

He was sick of driving, tired of the rotating shifts, fed up with dealing with domestics and drunks. Taking report after report. Nobody ever called a cop when they were having a great day.

Sure, there was plenty to like about being on the job. The ladies, for one thing. Known as badge bunnies. Little kids loved the uniform, acted like he was some kind of superhero. And there was the power that came with being a cop. Quentin was moderator, arbitrator, and sometimes judge and jury.

He hadn't reckoned with how much different it would be at a high school. Far from looking up to him, the students talked back, rolled their eyes, and made pig noises behind his back. He was six years older than the seniors, but they didn't seem to care he was their superior.

Three weeks into the school year, he spotted a girl walking down an otherwise empty corridor in the middle of a class period. She wore a long dress patterned with little purple flowers. Her wavy black hair hung past her waist, swaying with every step.

"Hey there," he called. "Shouldn't you be in class?"

She stopped and turned, pink rising in her cheeks, eyes still downcast. "I just had to go to the um, facilities. I asked permission."

Quentin reached her. She barely came to his shoulder. He loved her little stutter, her modesty, her nearly translucent skin. So many female students didn't hesitate to put themselves on display. To talk back.

"What's your name?" He gave her a gentle smile that hid his thoughts.

"Ruth. Ruth McCoy."

"I'm Officer Sinclair. I'm new here this year."

"I'm new, too." She peeped up at him through her dark lashes. Was she flirting? "I'm a freshman."

"I'll walk you back to class," Quentin said.

Even though neither said anything more, the silence between them seemed filled with promise.

As the days passed, he kept finding his eyes drawn to her. He soon figured out her schedule and made sure he was nearby. Once or twice a day, she would tell one of her teachers she needed to go to the bathroom. Out in the empty hall, they'd exchange a few sentences. They never spoke during passing times, but their eyes sought each other out. Occasionally, she flashed him a smile, there and gone before anyone could notice, and once, he winked and then watched the color rise in her face.

The other female students wore short skirts, tight leggings, and tops that revealed more than they concealed. But it was Ruth Quentin couldn't take his eyes off of. What was underneath all those long, loose layers? Once, he caught a glimpse of her knee as she gathered her ankle-length dress to walk up the stairs, and it was so much more exciting than the hundreds of knees he could see at any time.

He collected little crumbs of knowledge. She stood out in school, even if she didn't want the attention. According to the teachers, her family were members of a church called the Reapers of Divine Judgment. A cult, basically.

The teachers also said Ruth was smart, quiet, and lacking even the slightest familiarity with pop culture as well as art, music, or literature.

By the end of October, Quentin and Ruth were on a first-name basis. Both were careful never to be observed, but for different reasons. He knew he could lose his job. And she was afraid her parents would pull her out of school.

Her parents had seven children, and she was the oldest. Her mother, who had not been born into the church, had persuaded her husband to let the children go to school. It was frowned on but not forbidden, at least for the elementary grades. He learned Ruth was the first to attend high school, but she wouldn't go any further.

College was on a long list of activities considered too worldly.

When the second trimester began, Ruth's class schedule included PE. Opted out by her mother, she was assigned some easy essays to work on in the library. But the librarian was on leave and the subs came and went.

So Ruth was able to slip into Quentin's office unobserved. He kept his desk drawer filled with candy for her sweet tooth—the church believed in plain, healthy food, and the only dessert allowed was fruit. They talked about everything. He showed her how a phone worked, how to look things up on the internet, how to send a text. She seemed as intrigued with computers as he was. He regaled her with stories about his time on patrol.

And the whole time, Quentin watched her. The way her eyes lit up when she was fascinated. The way she bit her lip when she concentrated. The way her fingers twisted a lock of hair when she was nervous. Whenever he got close to her, her breath caught. He grew increasingly bold, tucking a stray tendril behind her ear or even squeezing her hand.

Quentin was crossing lines, but Ruth was, too. She had told him the rules of her church, about their belief nothing should distract them from their faith.

Under his attention, Ruth bloomed. Her eyes were brighter and she laughed more often. He found himself sharing pieces of his life he'd never divulged to anyone: his lonely childhood, his violent father, his deep-seated conviction the world was going wrong.

He knew she was off-limits. Too young. Too naive.

It was why he had to have her.

Ruth was fourteen, but with a woman's body.

And his office door locked.

He wooed her in subtle increments, a step closer each day, like coaxing a wild animal until it ate from your hand.

KEISHA

Connection

KEISHA WAS STILL TAKING HER SEAT FOR THE morning meeting of the Phantom task force when an excited Sanjay crowed, "We've got him, guys! We've got him!"

At the head of the conference table, Shane raised a cautioning hand. "Well, not exactly," he said, but he was smiling. "Late last night, we were alerted that a strong match just showed up on the GEDmatch PRO portal." He paused, letting the tension build. "This young woman matches the Phantom at 3,485 centimorgans, or about fifty percent of his DNA. She's definitely his daughter."

A chorus of cheers and exclamations filled the

room as everyone began talking. Keisha's mind filled with a tangle of emotions. Excitement, relief, and a twinge of disappointment. The task force had been chasing dead ends for years. Keisha had secretly hoped she would be the one to finally figure out the puzzle, but now science had beaten her to the punch.

"Does the daughter know?" Lori asked.

"No," Shane said. "GEDmatch PRO is like a one-way mirror. First, it only lets us look at users who have opted in, which, luckily, she did. So we can see her, but she can't see us. Even the PRO side limits what we can see to her name, email, and how much DNA she shares. But that's enough. Her name is Tessa Lundgren. And lucky for us, only a few people have that name. One is an eighteen-year-old who lives right here in Portland."

He clicked a button, and a photo of a girl appeared on the screen behind him. She was classically pretty, with porcelain skin, dark hair, and deep brown eyes. "Tessa Lundgren is a senior at Ida B. Wells High."

As Keisha studied Tessa's photo, she felt a twinge. This poor girl's world was about to be turned upside down. On the other hand, it was likely her father was a monster at home as well as out in the world, and this arrest would prove the best thing for her.

"What do we know about her father?" Jessica asked.

Shane tapped another button. "This is Lars Lundgren." Tessa's photo was replaced by one of a middle-aged man with receding blond hair and blue eyes. "According to his driver's license, six feet tall and one-eighty-five."

"His body size wouldn't be threatening to the victims," Lori said. "That could work in his favor."

Shane looked down at his notes. "According to his social media accounts, he likes to take part in triathlons and that sort of thing. So he's fit."

"And this guy's generally attractive, but not so attractive he's memorable," Jessica observed. "How old is he?"

"Forty-six."

Putting him in his late twenties for his first kill. Had he started with assault and worked his way up? "Does he have a record?" Keisha asked.

Shane shrugged. "Nothing except for a couple of speeding tickets nearly twenty years ago."

"What about his employment history?" Noah asked. "Anything that would have given him access to the victims?"

Shane pursed his lips. "He's a mechanical engineer, so there's no obvious connection."

"An engineer would have above-average intelligence and be orderly." Noah leaned forward. "And we know this guy is smart and takes care not to leave a mess."

Sanjay said, "And I'm guessing that at his job, nobody's watching him every second. He might even have to travel to jobsites."

"Maybe the connection is through his workouts?" Lori suggested. "He sees them at the gym or when he's out for a run. Maybe that's how Rachel Rule got on his radar."

Keisha looked back at the photo of Lars Lundgren, studying his unremarkable features. He looked so . . . normal. Still, there was a lot that fit their profile. Employed. Educated. A family. Of course, the same was true of many men. But their DNA hadn't been found on a murder victim's body.

Shane consulted his notebook. "We pulled up the other occupants of the home. It's him;

his wife, Lena; and an eleven-year-old daughter named Phoebe. Plus, of course, Tessa."

"He looks like a nice suburban dad," Lori said. "I can see how a woman might trust him, at least for a minute or two."

"A nice suburban dad who wants to put his hands around your throat," Jessica said.

"Don't they all," Lori agreed with a laugh.

"Do you think he knows his daughter took the test?" Keisha asked.

"I'm guessing not, or he would have tried to stop it."

"What's the plan?" Noah asked. "We can't just go knocking on his door."

Shane nodded. "Right. We need to tread carefully. If we spook him, he could run." He paused, his gaze sweeping the room. "But we can't get an arrest warrant based on his daughter's DNA. Just because he's raising her doesn't prove he's her father. The mother could have had an affair. So the first thing we need to do is surveil him and snag his DNA. We'll have teams watching him at work, at home, at his gym. Wherever he goes, we'll have eyes on him. And as soon as he spits out a piece of gum or tosses a water bottle, we'll nab it."

You didn't need a warrant to get someone's DNA, not if they discarded it. At that point, they no longer had an expectation of privacy. Lawyers could argue all day it violated the Fourth Amendment of the US Constitution, which protected Americans from unreasonable search and seizure. But so far, courts had not seen it that way.

Shane smiled with grim satisfaction. "We will have him under round-the-clock surveillance. And we'll wait for him to give us what we need."

October 9

I promised not to talk to boys, but
this is different. And I know I can
trust him. He's so easy to talk to. We
discuss everything, and not always
serious stuff. Today one of his jokes
had me laughing so hard I snorted!
And then we both laughed even
harder.

I can't stop thinking about how his
eyes crinkle when he smiles.

October 19

When he looks at me, I feel like I'm
the only person who matters. He
listens to my dreams and fears, and I
don't feel so lost and lonely anymore.

October 23

He almost kissed me today. At
least I think so. His face was so close

to mine. My heart felt like it was
about to burst. He stepped back and
apologized, but it didn't feel wrong
at all.

I know the church says we should
not be yoked with unbelievers. But
my own mother became a believer
because of my father.

But the reverse could have
happened. My mom could have
persuaded my dad to leave the
church. And then we would have had
birthdays and Christmases. Parties
and plays. Books and TV and movies.
If that had happened, I would be a
normal girl now, wearing makeup
and pants, with my hair brushing my
shoulders instead of my hips.

October 28

When I was younger, things were
so simple. I would marry, settle
down, and live near my parents with

my husband. I would cook, clean, and
raise our children in the church.

Now I'm not sure what I want.
Except him.

November 2

It's the start of the new trimester.
My schedule included PE. With boys.
My mom wrote a letter excusing me. As
a Reaper, I'm not allowed to wear
shorts or short-sleeve shirts, and I
certainly couldn't risk touching boys
as we jostled for a ball or something.

Maybe the me of two months ago
would have chafed at being set apart,
yet again.

But the new me realized I'm going
to have a whole period where no one
notices what I do. The PE teacher told
me to spend class time at the library,
researching and writing essays about
famous female athletes. She was
clearly irritated at having to think of

an alternative for me, so I'm sure she
has no real interest in reading my
reports.

The librarian is on maternity leave.
The series of replacements can barely
keep the books shelved. They won't
notice if one quiet girl is there or not
on any given day.

November 9

Something happened today. If
my parents knew, if anyone knew,
I would be pruned back for sure.
Maybe even uprooted.

November 22

Today Pastor Nolan talked about
sin. About how it can seem so
enticing, a sweet fruit hanging low on
the tree. He talked about temptation
and the fall from grace. It was like he
was speaking directly to me. A shiver
ran down my spine.

I looked around at the other girls in the congregation, their faces pure and innocent. I wondered how many harbored secrets like mine.

December 18

In the outside world, in a week it will be Christmas. For Reapers, it will be just another Friday. Reapers look at the Christmas tree and Santa Claus and all the decorations and see no evidence of Christ, but rather pagan traditions.

Our mother's relatives, who are not Reapers, still send us Christmas cards, even though we haven't seen them in person for years. While we are allowed to keep them, our parents tell us to lay them flat. Standing them up is too flashy.

Once, when I was about five, my mother took me, Jared, and Naomi to her parents' house a few days before Christmas. She warned us to pay no attention to the worldly trappings that would be on display. But when my grandmother opened the door, it was like a wonderland. The Christmas tree was decorated with shining lights and colorful glass balls. The house smelled of pine and cinnamon.

Grandpa cut us each a slice of a cake topped with sugar and cinnamon. It was the sweetest thing I had ever tasted. I ate my share, and then when no one was looking, sneaked some of Naomi's. Behind me, my mother was arguing with her parents, but I was concentrating on eating every last sweet crumb. I do remember hearing the word *cult*. It might have been the first time, but certainly not the last. Now I hear it every day, whispered at school.

The present my grandparents gave me—a book about a girl named Heidi—went into the garbage can as soon as we got home. So did everything else they gave us. That was the last time I ever got a present.

Until today. He handed me a small box tied with a golden ribbon. Inside were four chocolate truffles, each decorated in a different way. They came from a special store that sells only chocolates, and he picked out each one just for me. He said he had wanted to get me something more permanent, but realized it wouldn't be safe, at least not right now.

And then he made me forget all about the chocolate. About how we wouldn't see each other for seventeen whole days.

December 27

The most awful thing happened today. Stacy Carpenter has been uprooted. She is nineteen and got married last year. But the elders say she committed the sin of adultery, and now she is to be shunned. She tried to come into church this morning. She cried and begged, shouting she was sorry. But her parents, her brothers and sister, and even her husband didn't look at her at all. They turned away with stony faces and entered the church without looking back.

The elders linked their arms and denied her entrance. It was bad enough when she tried to push past them, but it was worse when she fell to her knees, weeping. Her face was wet and red. Once we were all inside, the elders closed the doors.

I could be Stacy. I'm not sure if they would uproot me, not when I'm fourteen, but they could definitely prune me back. Then I would be withdrawn from school and shut up

in my room until the elders decide
I'm truly repentant.

Some people are shut up for weeks.
Even months.

January 3

For the past two weeks, I haven't
spoken to him. Haven't seen him, not
even a glimpse. At first, he was all I
could think about. But the longer we
have been separated, the more I have
had time to think.

Our love is true. I know it. But I
also know I am powerless. I won't
be eighteen for over three years, and
until then my parents have charge of
me. They could break me. Or let the
elders do it.

January 4

He didn't believe me when I said it
was over. Not at first. He tried to hold
me, but I pulled away.

From now on, I'm going to act like what we did never happened. There will be nothing in my demeanor or even my thoughts to betray me. There are times I feel sick to my stomach about what I've done. But I have to be strong.

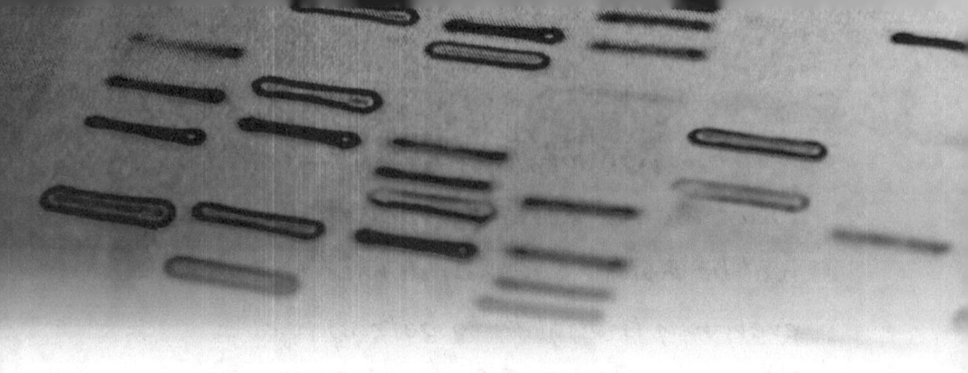

QUENTIN

Lies

Eighteen years earlier

QUENTIN WAS ONLY A WEEK INTO HIS SECOND YEAR as a school resource officer when he returned to his office after the last bell and found Ruth waiting for him. At the sound of the door opening, her head jerked up and she turned to face him. Her face was paler than he'd ever seen it, her hair looked greasy, and a fine tremble was washing over her. It had been eight months since she had last been here.

He kicked the door closed, glad most of the students and staff were already gone.

"Ruth, what are you doing here?" He had missed those secret meetings in his office. There had been a few other girls since she had broken things off, but none as sweet. He opened his arms.

She stepped back, her dark eyes filled with an expression he couldn't name. "Something happened today."

"Oh?"

"I felt so sick this morning I had to stay home. My stomach hurt so bad. I even started to think I might be dying. Like I had cancer or something."

Quentin folded his arms, glad she hadn't given in to his embrace. Working at a school was already too much of a germ fest for him to risk coming down with a bug. "I'm sorry to hear that."

"But I wasn't sick. I was having a baby. Right on our bathroom floor at home."

His mind went momentarily blank before reality seeped in. He stared at Ruth, a mix of disbelief and disgust churning inside him. His index finger tugged at the collar of his shirt as the small room turned claustrophobic.

With an effort, he kept his voice low. "A baby? What are you talking about?"

Her expression transformed, her eyes filling with joy. "She has all this dark hair, just like yours, and her eyes look like, like"—her words stumbled—"like she's seen infinity. Like she knows so much."

A baby. Was Ruth mentally ill? "And where is this 'baby'?"

"I cleaned her up, wrapped her in my night-gown, and took her to the fire station. I left her in the shade by the big door."

Quentin was starting to believe. And the more he did, the more anger swelled in his veins. "Does anyone else know about this?"

"No. I wore my mom's sun hat and a big coat when I was walking there. Then I came home and cleaned everything up."

"Does anyone else know you were pregnant?"

"*I* didn't even know. My stomach has been upset for months. I was barely eating." Ruth's mouth dropped open as the implications of what she had done sank in. "I hope I didn't hurt her by doing that. I thought it was probably cancer. I figured it was my fault for sinning."

He spit the words at her. "So whose baby is it, Ruth?"

"Yours, of course." Her eyes were big. Her lying eyes.

"It can't be mine." He resisted the urge to slap her. So he hadn't been good enough for her, but she had willingly laid down for someone else. It must be someone at her crazy church. He had kept his eye on her at school for months, but she never made friends, never talked to anyone, just kept her head down when she walked through the halls, a pale ghost in an oversize shroud.

"But we never used, um, protection." Two spots of red appeared in Ruth's pale cheeks. "I've heard if you don't, you can get pregnant."

"We didn't need to. I can't have children. So you should stop lying to me. I had cancer when I was a kid. I'll never be a father." Saying the words was like ripping off chunks of his own flesh. "If you're a mother, I didn't make you one. So who really put that baby in your belly?"

Ruth turned her face away as if she had been slapped. Then she took a deep, shuddering breath and turned back to him. "You did. There hasn't been anyone else. I love you." She looked up at him with pleading eyes. "I packed up some clothes. You can go back to the fire station with me. We can tell them I made a mistake. We can get her back. And then we'll go from there."

Through gritted teeth, he said, "Enough, Ruth. Stop lying to me. Stop with these fantasies."

"But I'm not lying." She raised her chin.

This girl he'd trusted, considered pure and innocent, had lied to him. Had it all been an act from the beginning? And now she was trying to draw him into the trouble she had created. "Leave me out of your lies, Ruth. Whatever happened to you had nothing to do with me."

"But you said you loved me. You said I was special." She raised her hands as if to pull him close. He raised his hands, too, but only to wrap them around her neck.

Her eyes widened, and for a long moment she was still, too weak and too shocked to fight back.

And when she finally struggled, it was too late.

KEISHA

Evidence

SINCE MIDDAY FRIDAY, THEY HAD BEEN SURVEIL-
ling Lars Lundgren. Now it was Tuesday evening, but he had yet to leave anything behind
they could test for DNA.

He had spent his time either at home or at
work or driving between them. He hadn't gone
out for lunch or to run an errand. Once he was
home, he stayed home. And despite how he presented himself online, he hadn't even gone for a
run or to the gym.

To limit the chance of Lundgren clocking his
tail, two cars were assigned to him at any given
time. They took turns being closer and rotated
the vehicles they used. Everyone on the task

force was pulling twelve-hour shifts to make it possible.

This afternoon, Shane Morrison had asked Keisha to partner with him. Her, the most junior member. She had worked hard to keep her expression impassive and only nodded, willing herself not to notice the expression on a few of the others' faces.

They had begun by following Lundgren from his job back to his house and then parking halfway down the block. The other team was around the corner.

Now Keisha sat in the passenger seat of an old black Nissan, peering through binoculars at Lundgren's house. The sun was starting to set, casting an orange glow over the neighborhood. She shifted in her seat, trying to subtly stretch her stiff legs.

Most of the house's windows were obscured by curtains or blinds. Only the large front windows allowed her to look in, but wherever Lundgren was, it wasn't the living room. Tessa and her sister, Phoebe, were sitting on the couch, watching television. Lena Lundgren entered the room and began talking, her hands moving animatedly.

The younger girl's attention didn't waver from the TV, while Tessa's mouth moved occasionally.

As she adjusted the focus wheel, Keisha had an unsettling thought. "Do you think this is what he does when he's planning a kill? Sits outside and watches?"

"Probably," Shane agreed. "At least enough to know when the victim will be alone. Some people think it's just luck he hasn't been caught yet, but nobody gets lucky eight times."

"If he's that alert, do you worry he'll notice us?"

"He might be starting to feel invincible." Shane rubbed his neck as if trying to unkink it. "Plus, I've got the daytime officers doing stuff that looks more normal than a guy just sitting in a car for no obvious reason."

"Like what?"

"Eating lunch or miming reading a book. When I've been on stakeout, I've put up flyers or pretended to fix my car. Once, I even put on a hard hat and an orange vest and took photos and measurements at an intersection."

"That's a good one." A woman working on a car might actually attract attention, but a stroller with a "sleeping" baby might work.

"A clipboard, a hard hat, and an orange vest can make you look nonthreatening."

Shane had switched from his POV to the Phantom's, the way Keisha had. "You ever hear that theory," she heard herself say. "That cops have more in common with criminals than they do with civilians?" What was she doing? This was not a conversation she should be having with her boss's boss.

"You mean the idea we're the sheepdogs, the bad guys are the wolves, and the general public is the sheep?" She waited for Shane to disparage it, but instead he said, "I think there's more than some truth to that."

A movement inside the house caught her eye. Keisha raised her binoculars again. Lundgren had entered the living room, and the girls were getting to their feet.

"It looks like everyone's leaving."

Shane keyed his mic and alerted the other team. As he did, the family was walking out to their car, a newer Toyota.

The two cars followed them, taking turns being the leader. A mile later, Lundgren pulled into a strip mall and stopped in front of a Pizzicato, a local chain of pizza restaurants.

Excitement buzzed in Keisha's veins. Pizza was perfect, just as long as Lundgren wasn't one of those overly thorough people who ate every bite of the crust, even the bare rind. Pizza crust was like a sponge for DNA.

Shane parked in front of a pottery-painting place four doors down and turned to Keisha. "I want you to go in."

"Me?"

"Of the four of us, you look least like a cop." He reached into the back seat, snagged a plain black ball cap, and handed it to her. "Go in, order something, sit near them if you can, and keep an eye on everything he touches, eats, or drinks. As soon as he leaves, your job is to collect it." He reached past her knees and opened the glove box. Inside was an actual box of gloves. Blue latex ones. "Take a couple of these with you."

She squeezed the ball cap over her curls, stuffed the gloves into her pocket, and walked inside. The Lundgrens had already ordered. Lena was paying while Lars and the two girls walked back to a table. Lars moved a little stiffly, as if he were tired.

Next to them was an empty table. A man was

hovering by the display case, clearly waiting his turn to order. Not making eye contact, Keisha cut in front of him. "I'll have a combo slice and a Diet Coke." She ignored the huffing noise the other customer made behind her.

"For here or to go?"

"Here." She grabbed the number the cashier handed over. At the empty table, she took the seat facing Lars Lundgren, then took out her phone. Staring at your phone was the best way to blend in, and if she was discreet, Keisha might be able to snap a few photos. The other teams had gotten video of him, but at a distance.

The tantalizing aroma of baking pizza made her mouth water despite the circumstances. "Seated at next table," she texted Shane.

Over the top of her phone, she kept her eyes on Lars. So this was the man. You never knew, did you? Tall, slender, even slight. He might not even outweigh her. Chinos and a loose pale blue button-down with the sleeves rolled up.

She studied his facial expressions, the way he interacted with Tessa and Phoebe, looking for signs he was the monster they suspected him to be. But all she saw was an ordinary man—perhaps slightly tense, but that could be attributed to anything. You wouldn't give him a second glance.

The parents took turns talking to their daughters, but Keisha eventually realized they weren't talking to each other. When the pizza came, Lena distributed it onto white ceramic plates while Lars scanned his surroundings. Then he turned toward Keisha. As his eyes, ringed with dark circles, met hers, she felt a jolt.

He pointed at a shaker on her table. "Could I borrow those hot red pepper flakes?" His voice sounded hoarse. Maybe he was sick or had been.

"With your stomach?" Lena interjected. "Is that such a good idea?"

He didn't reply, just held out his hand, his eyes on Keisha.

She handed over the shaker. Keisha hadn't been this aware of the brush of someone's hand since seventh grade. She was probably burned now. You wouldn't want Lars wondering why the same young woman kept showing up at the same places he did.

He shook it heavily over the slice. Was he adding a few extra shakes to spite his wife? But perhaps he had overdone it, because he ate only a couple of bites before he put his slice down with a sigh. When her pizza arrived, Keisha picked it up to look like she was eating, but she only nibbled at it.

The girls had wolfed their way through several slices, and Lena had eaten two when Lars said, "You guys ready to go?"

They pushed their chairs back. As soon as the door closed behind them, Keisha was up, yanking on the gloves and snatching up his half-eaten slice. Shane hurried in, carrying several brown paper bags, folded so the word EVIDENCE printed in big block letters wasn't visible. You used paper for anything with moisture, because in plastic it could degrade or even mold.

Lundgren's straw went into a second bag. Then Keisha picked up the half-empty glass of water he had been drinking, decanted it into his wife's glass, and put the glass into a third bag.

Only then did she notice a busboy holding a wet bar rag staring at them. But Keisha didn't say anything and Shane didn't either. They just walked out to the car and sped straight for the lab.

224

Maxwell Holloway's intense gaze seems to bore into the viewer. "Two years went by while the city of Portland grappled with a growing sense of dread. Then another victim was claimed by the shadows. Passion Flower, a trans woman who, in choosing her new name, sought a semblance of beauty in a world tainted by darkness. Her short life became another tragic chapter in the Portland Phantom's relentless spree."

The camera cuts to a montage of Passion Flower, a striking woman with large dark eyes and high cheekbones.

"Passion was found lifeless in her car. At first, authorities believed it was a hate crime. Eventually, they noticed a watch buckled around her wrist. It was the same brand Bettina Martinez had worn. DNA testing confirmed their hunch." Holloway drops his voice. "And it was even more disturbing when homicide detectives noticed one of Passion's silver earrings was gone. They knew when they found that earring, it would be on another victim."

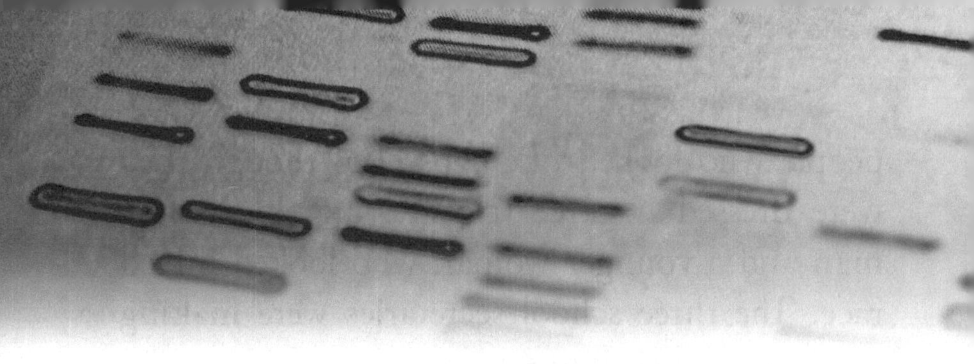

TESSA

Secrets

AN ANNOUNCEMENT CRACKLED FROM THE SPEAKER overhead just as biology was about to start. "Tessa Lundgren, please come to the office." It was a week after she had met Jared and two days after he had given Tessa her mom's diary.

Victor raised an eyebrow. "Are you in trouble?" he whispered.

"Of course not." Then she thought of her family. Had something happened to one of them? A car accident, a heart attack? A wave of panic propelled her down the hallway.

The vice principal, a woman Tessa only knew from assemblies and announcements, stood in the doorway of the office. Next to her were two people who looked like cops even though they were dressed in street clothes: an older white man and a younger woman who looked mixed race. The three school secretaries were making no secret of their interest.

"Tessa, these two police officers are here to speak to you," the vice principal said.

Whatever came next, Tessa sensed she could never go back. "What's wrong?" She tried to imagine Phoebe, her mom, her dad, erased from this world. She would be like an astronaut untethered from their ship, floating away in empty space.

The woman stepped forward. "Nothing's wrong. We wanted to speak with you because you might have some information that could be useful to us on a case."

"Let's talk in here." The man gestured to a small room normally used for misbehaving students. Tessa took one of the four plastic chairs at the round table. As the woman took the seat next to her, he closed the door.

"I'm Detective Shane Morrison," he said, "and this is Officer Keisha Washington. And just to confirm, Tessa, you are eighteen?"

228

She nodded, still braced, but not knowing for what. "Am I in trouble?"

Detective Morrison's smile was professional as he took a seat on Tessa's other side. "No. Not at all. You can leave at any time. But we're hoping you can help us."

Officer Washington leaned forward over clasped hands. Her partner had crow's-feet and silver temples, but this woman didn't look much older than Tessa.

"Tessa, we're here because we need your help in identifying a person connected to an ongoing investigation. We believe you might have valuable information that could assist us." She took out a notebook and pen. "What do you know about your parents?"

"Do you mean my adoptive parents or my biological parents?" Tessa was already shifting her calculus of doom.

The two detectives exchanged a glance, but she couldn't read their expressions.

Officer Washington said, "You're adopted? The Lundgrens aren't your biological parents?"

"They adopted me when I was a newborn. I've always been curious about my birth parents, so a friend gave me an Ancestry DNA kit for my birthday."

Detective Morrison said, "And then you posted your genetic information from Ancestry on another site called GEDmatch." It wasn't a question.

Officer Washington's voice was soft. "And when you did, we were alerted you were a match to someone."

All the air left the room. When she signed up for GEDmatch, Tessa had clicked on the box allowing law enforcement to use her DNA to figure out the identity of violent criminals or unidentified bodies. They must be talking about Ruth. She had been reading and rereading her mom's journal ever since Jared had given it to her. The person who wrote those pages seemed so young, so innocent. So naive.

Now tears pricked the back of her eyes. "My mom. It's my mom, isn't it?"

Officer Washington's head tilted. "So you know who your mom is?"

Under the table, Tessa dug her fingernails into her thighs, trying to steady herself. "I figured it out through my Ancestry results. Her name is Ruth McCoy." Should she have said it *was* Ruth McCoy?

"And what do you know about her?" Officer Washington wrote down Ruth's name.

"She was fourteen when she got pregnant with me, and fifteen when I was born. She managed to keep it a secret from everyone. After she gave birth to me, she wrapped me in a nightgown, left me at a fire station, and took off." Tessa was trying to delay the inevitable by building a wall of words. "Her family never looked for her because they're part of this weird culty church called the Reapers of Divine Judgment and they cut off anyone they think is too, quote, worldly."

Officer Washington scribbled furiously. Detective Morrison was also making notes, but not as many.

"My biological mother is dead, isn't she?" Tessa could picture it: A girl three years younger than Tessa was now standing next to the freeway with her thumb out. Running away before anyone figured out what she had done. Dressed like an extra on *Little House on the Prairie*. Looking like the perfect victim.

Officer Washington raised her head. Her dark eyes met Tessa's. "Dead?" she echoed.

"I've been trying to find her, but she's left no trace. I've checked every social media site, tried googling different versions of her name, but there's nothing. I talked to one of her brothers who also left the church, and in all these years, he's never heard from her. You're trying to use my DNA to identify a body, right?" Tessa took a deep breath. "So if this unidentified body matches me, she's my mother. Ruth McCoy."

"Tessa, we didn't know anything about your mother until just now." Officer Washington's voice was almost gentle. "The person we're actually trying to find out more about is your father. Do you know his name?"

"Wait. So my biological mom is okay?"

Detective Morrison pressed his lips together. "As far as we know. It's your father we're asking about."

The kaleidoscope shifted, forming another pattern. "So how did he die? Was he murdered?"

The two cops looked at each other.

"What? What aren't you telling me," Tessa

demanded. It felt as if she were on a roller coaster that wouldn't stop.

"We don't know his name or much about him," Officer Washington said. "Although having your mother's name should help us figure those things out."

Detective Morrison leaned forward. "But even though we don't know his name, we do know something about him." He paused. "Have you heard of the Portland Phantom?"

"Of course. He just killed that girl, Alida somebody. Killed a bunch of girls before." Tessa realized what they were implying. Her dad must be another victim. "But I've never heard of him killing any guys."

"Your biological father's DNA was left at the scene of one of the Phantom's murders," Detective Morrison said.

It took a minute for it to sink in. What they were saying wasn't true. It couldn't be true. They were saying her father, the man she had dreamed of finding, was a serial killer.

"How do you even know I'm related to this guy?" There had to be some mistake. After all,

Tessa had originally thought Gina was her mother, and that turned out to be wrong.

Officer Morrison said, "You share almost exactly fifty percent of his DNA. There's only one possible explanation for that high a percentage. He's definitely your father."

TESSA

Famous

TESSA HAD BEEN SO STUNNED BY THE REVELATION about who her father was, or had become, that she hadn't thought to tell the cops about her mother's diary. When she got home, she read it again, looking for clues and not finding any. A few times, she attempted to go online and read about her biological father. But it was too much, and she just picked up the diary again.

The next day, she took the diary to school, and Victor and El read it over lunch, sitting side by side, with El turning the pages. When they finished, they looked across the table at her.

"There are no clues," Tessa said. "Not his name, not a description." She felt a flare of disgust, not at her father, but at Ruth. "It sounded like she thought she loved him. She was so gullible."

"Growing up the way she did kept her pretty sheltered," El countered. "That's probably why he sought her out. Because she was innocent. She didn't have any life experience. Her parents and that cult slash church of hers made sure of that."

"Your mom might have been way too young," Victor said, "but she was strong. Strong enough to give you a better life. Strong enough to leave behind everything she knew and make a new life for herself."

The next night was a Friday. El's parents were at a banquet, meaning the three of them could watch the two-year-old Lifetime documentary *Chasing Shadows: The Hunt for the Portland Phantom* without any adult questions or comments.

"Are you sure you're up for this?" Victor asked Tessa. He was sitting on one side of the family's old leather couch. El was in the kitchen, making popcorn.

Unable to sit still, Tessa was pacing in front of the TV. "I need to know more, but I can't deal with it by myself. Even reading the Wikipedia entry was almost too much."

For the last two days, El and Victor had immersed themselves in articles, websites, and innumerable TikToks about the Portland Phantom. Tessa, on the other hand, had been rendered almost immobile. She had grown up hearing the Phantom referenced as an all-purpose boogeyman in playground games and at slumber parties. At the same time, with the long lulls between kills, it had been easy to forget about him, at least until he struck again.

Now, El came into the living room carrying a big yellow bowl. "Have you called that Officer Washington yet?" she asked.

"I'm going to." When Victor gave her a skeptical look, she added, "I swear."

El sat on the other end of the couch and patted the middle cushion while looking at Tessa. She forced herself to sit. El plopped the warm bowl of popcorn into her lap, but Tessa couldn't imagine trying to eat a single kernel.

El picked up the remote. "Are you ready?"

Tessa nodded. Her breathing felt stuck.

The screen showed a quick montage of famous Portland scenes. Victor said, "All the classics."

A man's smooth, deep voice said, "A dark

secret lurks in the quiet corners of Portland, Oregon. Once known for its serene landscapes and hipster havens, the city is now haunted by the Portland Phantom, who has murdered seven young women over the last fourteen years."

They were talking about her dad, Tessa thought, shocked all over again. They were talking about the man she had wondered about forever, had pictured in a hundred different ways.

She shot El a sad smile. "Didn't we always say my dad was probably someone famous?"

The documentary had the usual: a smarmy host, a variety of talking heads, stilted reenactments. The narrator seemed almost gleeful as he spoke over images of shadowy figures and dramatized crime scenes. Before tonight, Tessa and El had watched at least a dozen of these types of shows, but just as entertainment. Sad and scary, to be sure, but also a little bit fun. Now the horrific events depicted on-screen were as close as the blood in Tessa's veins. The world called the Phantom a monster. But if her mom hadn't given her up, would she now be thinking of him as "Dad"?

"This thing is cheesy." El snorted before grabbing a handful of popcorn.

While the story was tacky, it was also true. These women were dead. And it was all because of her father.

When the documentary finished, El turned off the TV.

Tessa got to her feet. "My mom was just a kid, and my dad is this horrible killer." She had no place to put the emotions roiling within her, so she took them out on El. "I wish you had never gotten me that stupid DNA test."

El flinched.

Tessa blinked and felt a hot tear run down her face.

Victor grabbed her wrist. "Breathe, Tessa," he said in a low voice. "You're not breathing."

It was work to drag the air in. Her chest felt like a block of wood.

"Good. Now do it again."

Instead of following his directions, she pulled free from his grasp. Her hand was almost the size of Victor's. Since her mom had been petite, Tessa's hands must have come from her dad. What else had she inherited? Was she destined to turn bad?

"It's been two years since they made that."

She rubbed a spot between her eyebrows where a headache was starting. "And it seems like they don't know anything more than they did. Except where Rachel's driver's license ended up. It feels like they're never going to catch him."

Victor waved his hand at the now dark TV. "This documentary must have made the Phantom happy. It made him seem all powerful *and* a complete mystery."

"Do you remember Greek mythology from ninth grade?" El asked. "If you want to make the monster disappear, you can't just push it away. Hiding in the darkness is how they get more powerful."

Something clicked into place for Tessa. "Like the monsters in *Stranger Things*. They were so much scarier in the first season when you couldn't see them."

"The Phantom is just a man, not a monster," Victor said. "And a man can be stopped."

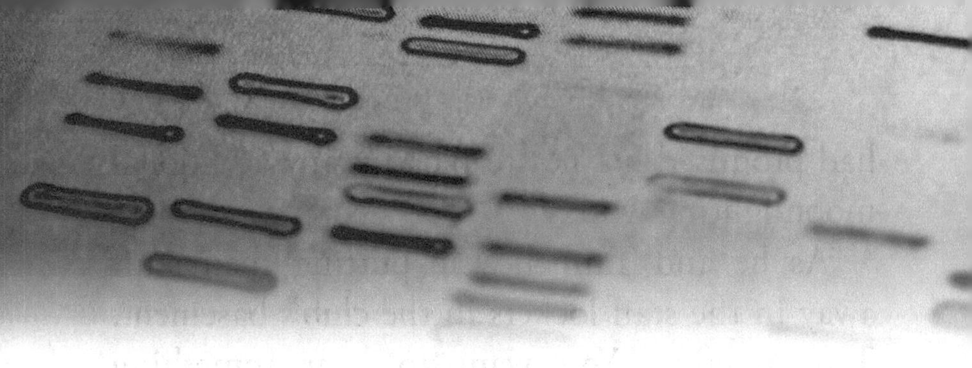

QUENTIN

Churning

AFTER A QUICK DINNER WITH MELANIE FRIDAY night, Quentin had driven back downtown to work at the club. Ever since Alida's murder, he could have moonlighted every night if he wanted to. The whole city was on edge. Talking about the Phantom was like an itch Quentin couldn't stop scratching. Luckily for him, every Portlander was on the same page, especially near a college campus filled with young women.

But in an ironic twist, the latest killing had also unsettled his own wife. Melanie hated it when he went out at night and could not bring herself to go to bed until he came home. So he had promised her not to pick up any additional moonlighting work.

As he and Tanner were putting their stuff away in the staff lockers in the club's basement, Tanner said, "You want to hear something crazy?" Quentin wasn't so sure he did, until Tanner added, "About the Phantom."

Quentin froze.

"They're holding it pretty close to the vest, but it turns out the Phantom actually has a kid. A daughter. Only she knows nothing about her dad. She was adopted."

Now even his thoughts went still. "How do they know she's his kid?" he finally managed to say.

"She did a DNA test on Ancestry and then eventually put the results on GEDmatch. The department uses GEDmatch Pro for high-profile cases, so GEDmatch notified us immediately. At first, we thought the Phantom was the guy who's raising her, but then they found out she was adopted. So now we're basically back to square one."

"What about the mother?" Quentin kept his tone casual, even though he was suddenly picturing Ruth's black waterfall of hair, her pale skin, her lips a perfect cupid's bow.

"I guess they know the mother's name, but they haven't been able to locate her."

Quentin's thoughts were churning. He was a father. He had a child. Ruth hadn't lied.

He had spent the past eighteen years thinking about her betrayal. Obsessing about it. Punishing other women for her misdeeds.

But Ruth had told him the truth.

**From the Lifetime documentary
*Chasing Shadows: The Hunt for the Portland
Phantom***

There's a glint in Maxwell Holloway's eye.
"Two years go by before another victim
of the Portland Phantom is found. Long
enough the city begins to hope the monster
is gone. But then the body of Lindsey Turner
is found just inside her open front door.
She appears to have been in the process
of unloading her car. She had a stand at
Portland's famed Saturday Market, where
she sold her hand-knitted scarves, hats, and
mittens."

The screen switches to a photo of
woman with a messy dark bun standing
behind a long table under a white canopy.
She's grinning, her hands spread to
encompass the colorful items on display. All
are rainbow-colored, the universal symbol
for LGBTQ pride.

"Her body was discovered by her partner. And even though Lindsey didn't have pierced ears, she was found wearing a single silver earring."

QUENTIN

Clay

HE WAS A FATHER. *A FATHER.* QUENTIN KEPT RETURN-ing to the idea, until it crowded out all other thoughts.

Before he and Tanner had clocked out from the club, he had managed to get the other man to reveal the daughter's name. *His* daughter's name.

Tessa Lundgren. The first name like a whisper. And her last name simply wrong. It should have been Sinclair, the same as his.

A girl. He couldn't help being a little disappointed. A boy would probably have been like him, strong and disciplined and good with his hands. But a girl? Girls were soft. Trusting.

This girl was half his, but whom did she take

after? Did Tessa have Ruth's striking eyes or soft laugh? Or perhaps she was like Quentin, tall with dark hair?

Whenever Quentin decided to go on a mission, the first step was selecting the victim. The next was learning everything about them. He would become their shadow, watching them in secret, noting their habits, memorizing their routines. In some ways, this was always the best part. When it was still a fantasy, and he was filled with anticipation.

The same excitement bubbled up in him again, but with a difference. This girl wasn't a project, to be completed and then discarded. Tessa was his own flesh and blood.

When he got home, he went to bed at the same time as Melanie and waited until she was softly snoring. Then he quietly went back downstairs and unlocked his study door. Melanie believed he kept the room locked because he occasionally brought home confidential material from work. She was good about not asking questions.

After opening an anonymous browser, he typed "Tessa Lundgren" into the search bar.

He was lucky her name wasn't Jennifer Smith

or something equally common. Still, there were several to choose from, including women from California and Minnesota. But when he looked for results fitting *his* Tessa, he found only a couple.

A few years ago, *The Oregonian* had run a group photo of a half dozen middle schoolers planting trees for Earth Day. His daughter's head was tipped down as she pushed a trowel into the mud, so he couldn't see her face.

He also found what he thought was her Instagram account, but it was set to private, and her profile photo just showed a stack of books. He didn't recognize most of the titles.

These scraps did nothing to satisfy his curiosity. Where did she live? Who were her friends? Was she moving through the world with the same restlessness he had felt at her age?

From an online data broker that operated in the shadows and demanded payment in crypto, Quentin purchased Tessa's physical address, email address, and cell phone number.

He barely slept that night, already anticipating the first time he would see her. He told Melanie he was going to be gone all morning, running errands. Long before Tessa appeared, he was waiting in his car parked down the block from her house.

When she finally stepped out her front door, he felt an ache just beneath his breastbone. His gaze fastened on her while his fingers rubbed his chest. His first thought was she was beautiful, with dark wavy hair and pale skin that set off her dark eyes.

She began walking down the sidewalk in his direction, but on the other side of the street. Her head was up, her hands loose by her sides. She wore jeans, gray sneakers, and a caramel-colored sweater.

Quentin looked at Tessa and saw Ruth. He looked at her and saw himself. But the longer he looked, the more of himself he saw.

After she turned the corner, he started his car and reluctantly drove away. He reminded himself this was just the first day.

At work, the higher-ups didn't pay much attention to Quentin. They gave him free rein as long as parents and the city didn't complain, as long as there weren't bad stories about the university on the local news.

So for the next few days, he observed Tessa

before and after school. She spent a lot of time with two people. One was a girl with purple hair. What were her parents thinking?

The other was a brown-skinned boy. Quentin didn't like that. Not one little bit. To keep better tabs on him, he slipped a tracker under the rear bumper of his car. Through his binoculars or from behind a clipboard, Quentin saw how easy it was for this boy to make Tessa smile.

If Quentin had raised Tessa, would she be different? Would she be more careful of the company she kept? It was better to be like him. If you kept people at a distance, then you were less likely to be betrayed, less likely to be hurt.

At work, his mind often drifted into a reverie of what-ifs and might-have-beens. It was another part of his fantasy, one offering sanitized versions of his own darkness. And yet, he couldn't escape one fact: Tessa was also Ruth's daughter.

According to Tanner, the girl had been told about him. And Tessa, in turn, had told the cops Ruth's name, which, of course, was turning out to be a dead end. How did Tessa feel, knowing she had come from him? Was she scared? Or maybe a little bit curious?

This afternoon, Quentin was sitting at an outdoor table at a coffee shop near her school, his eyes hidden by sunglasses, wearing a beanie instead of the ball cap he had worn last time. He shifted uncomfortably in the metal chair, his unease growing as he watched Tessa walk by, only about ten feet away. She laughed at something that Hispanic boy had said and then tucked her hair behind one ear.

Quentin's fingers involuntarily clenched his coffee cup. He caught himself before he crushed it entirely. His daughter wasn't a flirt. She just hadn't been taught how to behave.

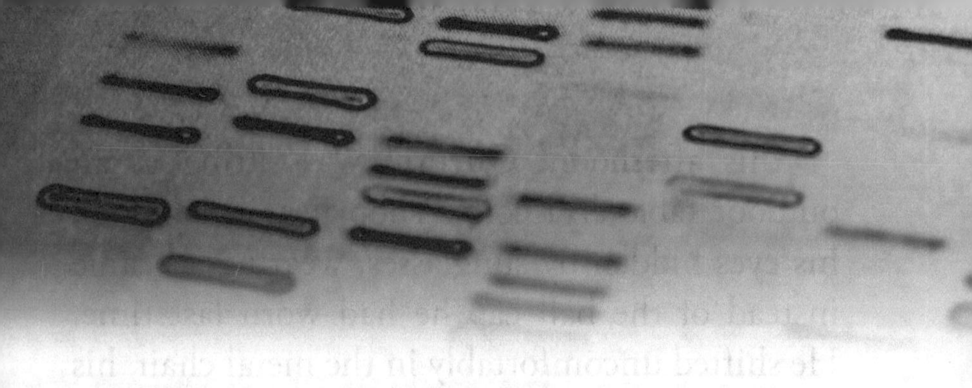

KEISHA

Safe

KEISHA AND NOAH HAD ARRANGED TO MEET JARED McCoy AT noon in the cafeteria at Montgomery Park, where he worked. As they rode up the escalator between wide sets of gleaming white stairs, the mingled scents of fryer oil and basil hung in the air.

Keisha craned her head. Far above, a glass ceiling revealed blue sky and puffy white clouds. As they reached the top of the escalator, she glanced around the atrium. On their left, a handful of people pushed red plastic trays down a cafeteria food line. The rest of the large open space was filled with several dozen tables, about a third of which were occupied.

A dark-haired man in his thirties got to his feet and waved. His navy dress pants and neatly pressed pale blue shirt were accented with a plaid bow tie. They wound their way back and shook hands while introducing themselves.

"You guys hungry?" Jared asked, nodding at the cafeteria. "The ziti's pretty decent." All he had in front of him was a white metal water bottle decorated with a rainbow sticker.

"We're good," Keisha said as she and Noah pulled out their notebooks. "Thank you for agreeing to meet with us."

"I figured better here than my office. People might have questions, and I haven't told anyone here about my past. The only way to understand the Reapers is to grow up one." In his features were echoes of both Tessa and the two photos Keisha had seen of Ruth.

"I've never been in this building." She looked up. The hallways on the floors above were open to the atrium. Keisha wondered if anyone had ever jumped from them, the kind of dark thought she didn't use to have before she joined the force.

Jared's voice broke her train of thought. "It used to be a Montgomery Ward warehouse.

Supposedly, the workers used roller skates to get around. It's why they called it Montgomery Park, because they had to change only two letters of the sign."

"And you're an accountant for a health insurance company, right?" Noah asked.

"I know it sounds boring, but," Jared began, "it really is."

Keisha smiled despite herself.

"I wanted something safe. And I figured everyone's always going to need accountants and health care."

"We spoke with your parents about your sister," Noah said.

Jared's laugh lacked any humor. "How did that go? Reapers aren't fond of law enforcement. Especially when it interferes with their more esoteric practices."

"They were pretty closemouthed," Keisha said diplomatically. Ruth's mother had gotten quieter and her father louder the longer they were there. An undertone to his questions and objections had made her think he would turn on his wife as soon as they left. "They said they haven't seen or heard from Ruth since the day she disappeared."

"Which was also the day Tessa was born," Jared said.

"They disputed that. Especially your father. He refused to believe Ruth had ever been pregnant." Keisha remembered the look in his eyes, disbelief fighting a growing certainty, even as he shouted that his daughter hadn't been a *whore*. "And your mother acted like the whole idea was news to her. She pretended Tessa and her friends hadn't been there before us, and we didn't contradict her."

Jared sighed heavily. "Thank you for that. Reapers aren't above using physical discipline, not just on children, but wives as well. 'Wives, submit to your husband as to the Lord.'"

"As the church submits to Christ," Noah added, supplying the end to what Keisha guessed was a Bible verse. She blinked. As far as she knew, Noah wasn't religious. His swearing was legendary.

"I'm sure it was a shock when you met Tessa," Keisha said.

Jared toyed with his water bottle's cap. "That's an understatement. Although I liked her. And her friends. And when she told me who she was,

I could see it. But if she's anything like Ruth, still waters run deep."

Noah leaned forward. "So you've had time to get used to the idea your sister had a baby. Have you given any more thought to who the father might be?"

Jared looked from Noah to Keisha and back again. "Are you guys thinking it was child abuse because Ruth was so young? Two detectives seem like a lot of manpower for such an old case."

Noah paused and then said, "It's more about *who* the father was."

His eyes widened. "Is Tessa's dad someone famous? Like a politician or something?"

"Or something," Keisha said dryly. She looked at Noah, who nodded. "We only know one fact about Tessa's father. He's the man the media calls the Portland Phantom."

Jared's mouth fell open. "What? That can't be right."

"We've been looking for him for years but hitting only dead ends," Noah said. "Then Tessa put her DNA on GEDmatch and we were alerted right away."

"GEDmatch?" Jared echoed. "That was my

boyfriend's suggestion since Tessa wasn't having any luck on Ancestry. I figured it had to be complicated, since Ruth was so young, but this... this is something else entirely."

"So do you have any ideas?" Keisha asked.

Jared shook his head. "It's like I told Tessa. Ruth was never alone with a man. Or a boy, for that matter. Our whole family went to church as a unit and she was never singled out by any of the elders."

"What about school?" Noah asked.

"Our parents actually let Ruth go to public high school for ninth grade. The next year, I got to go only the first few days, until Ruth ran away. Then they pulled me out and that was the end of that. But the year before, she walked the rest of us to the elementary school before she went on to Brookwillow. Then at the end of the day, we walked over and waited for her. So she couldn't have met anyone before or after school, and during school she would have been in class."

"Brookwillow?" Keisha murmured. "Why is that familiar?"

"They've got one of the best football teams in the country," Noah replied.

Keisha came up with a different answer. She sucked in her breath, then turned to Noah. "Where did Dana Jennings's son go to school?" Dana had been the first of the Phantom's kills.

He pointed his pen at her. "You're right! Brookwillow."

Keisha said, "That can't be a coincidence. He must have had some kind of connection to Brookwillow. A teacher or maybe a student."

"Or the custodian, even a parent." Noah scribbled in his notebook. "We're going to need to get our hands on their records."

"I went there for only about ten days," Jared said. "But I don't remember Ruth reacting to any of the teachers or, for that matter, the students. Although when I read her journal later, it was clear she had had some kind of a boyfriend the year before. She broke it off after she got worried our parents might lock her up in her room if they knew."

"Your sister kept a journal?" Keisha's heart sped up. "We need to see that."

He lifted his empty hands. "I gave it to Tessa Lundgren a week ago."

Tessa had told them about her newfound

uncle, but she said nothing about her mother's diary.

Jared looked from Noah to Keisha. "The one person who would definitely know who Tessa's father is is my sister. Have you been able to find Ruth?" Hope shone in his eyes.

Noah shook his head. "We've checked voting records, driver's license lists, death certificates, and other public records. No Ruth McCoy that matches. Not even a Ruth with a different last name and the same date of birth. Same with the initial *R* or just using her middle name. If she went into hiding, she's doing a good job of it."

"Maybe she figured out how evil this guy was," Jared said. "And she realized the only way to be safe was to get as far away as possible. Change her name, maybe even get off the grid."

But Keisha could tell from his expression he didn't believe his own words.

Noah gave her a look, and he knew they were all thinking the same thing.

Maybe Dana hadn't been the first victim.

Maybe it had been Ruth.

TESSA

Wrong

WHEN TESSA WALKED INTO HER HOUSE AFTER school Monday, she was surprised to hear voices. On one side of the dining room table were her parents. And on the other was the female cop who had come to her school last week and revealed the terrible truth about her father.

"What is *she* doing here?" The words burst out of her. Her biological father's identity was a dark secret she was still processing. It was one thing for El and Victor to know. But her parents? She had still been deciding how and when to tell them.

"Tessa!" her mom scolded.

"Officer Washington reached out to us," her

dad said. "She wanted to know if we had any information about your birth parents."

"Teens don't always share everything with their parents," the cop said. "I have to follow every possible lead."

"So, do they?" Tessa locked eyes with the other woman. "Know more?"

"No." Her expression changed. "But earlier today, we spoke with your uncle Jared. He told us that Ruth kept a diary and that he gave it to you last week. But you didn't mention it when we met."

"I was in shock." It was the truth, but by the way the cop tilted her head, Tessa thought she didn't believe her.

"Right now, Ruth's diary is the best chance we have of figuring out who your biological father is."

The man Tessa had always called Dad was sitting right there. But looking at his unsmiling, hollow-cheeked face, she didn't recognize him at all.

"There's nothing in it about that. It's clear Ruth was involved with someone, but she never names him, never even hints."

"We still need to examine it." Officer Washington reached into her shoulder bag and took out something like a brown paper grocery bag, only labeled *EVIDENCE* in block letters.

"I'll go get it." As soon as she was out of sight, Tessa sprinted up the stairs, already pulling her phone from her pocket. What were the chances she would ever get back the one thing tying her to her biological mother?

She pulled the notebook from its hiding place, laid it on the bed, and began taking pictures with her camera phone. *Click, flip, click, flip.* She squinted through tear-filled eyes to make sure the words were in focus.

"What are you doing?" The quiet question made her jump. Officer Washington was standing in the doorway with her hands on her hips.

"I figure I might not ever get it back." In Ruth's words, Tessa had found an echo of her own feelings and desires. A connection.

The cop didn't deny it. "I don't think you realize how important this is. This guy has been killing women for sixteen years. This diary might be the best lead we have. Maybe the only one."

"Like I said, it doesn't really say anything

about him. Just that she met him at school." Tessa looked back down and started taking pictures again. "It's mostly about how she wished things were different, her questions about her faith, how lonely she was." The word *lonely* came out half strangled. She imagined some middle-aged guy in a uniform leafing through the diary, bored by her mother's most intimate thoughts.

"I know it must seem like an invasion of privacy." Officer Washington's tone was unapologetic.

"I feel like I just got my mom back and now you're taking her from me." Tessa turned to the last page, snapped a picture, and shut the notebook. She held it out to the cop, who took it without a word and slipped it inside the evidence bag before going downstairs.

Tessa waited until the front door closed. After sinking onto her bed, she pulled a pillow against her chest and cried. She thought maybe her mom—or the woman she had always called Mom—might come upstairs to check on her, but no one did. Finally, she gathered her courage and went downstairs.

Her parents were still sitting at the dining

room table, talking in low tones. For a second, they looked like strangers. She must have made some small noise, because they both turned to her.

"Oh, Tessa," her dad said haltingly. "Why didn't you come to us? Why didn't you tell us what you were doing?" He didn't look angry. He looked sad.

"Because I didn't want to hurt your feelings." And it would definitely hurt them if they ever learned how many times she had imagined different parents. Maybe even better parents.

Her mother shook her head. "Did you think you could keep this a secret from us forever?"

A red tide rose in Tessa at her parents' hypocrisy. It was easier to be angry than to be sad or guilty, and she welcomed the energy swelling in her veins. "You guys are ones to talk. You have your secrets you never talk to me about. Do you think I haven't noticed all your 'meetings' "—she made air quotes—"and how stressed you guys look all the time? At night, I hear you arguing. And Dad's been sleeping on the couch. So when were you planning on telling us the truth?"

"The truth about what?" her dad asked, his voice cracking.

"About how you're getting a divorce?"

Her dad's head jerked back. "Is that what you think is going on?"

Her mom pressed her lips together and shook her head. "Haven't you noticed how your dad's been losing weight?"

Tessa had and she hadn't. She half remembered times he had pushed a nearly full plate of food away. "I thought he was just on a diet." But now when she looked at him, really looked, she saw his hollow cheeks, his sunken eyes.

"Something's wrong with Lars," her mom said. "He's been running fevers. Every night, he gets these terrible headaches. He tosses and turns, so he's been sleeping on the couch so he doesn't keep me awake. And he's lost twelve pounds."

"Sixteen," he corrected. "I try to eat, but I'm lucky if I can force down one or two mouthfuls." His sigh was so deep it shook.

"What's wrong?" Tessa's question came out nearly as a whisper.

Her mom answered. "Nobody knows. It doesn't help that it took two weeks to get an appointment. They did a bunch of tests, but they just raised more questions. His sedimentation rate is elevated, there's microscopic blood in his urine, and his liver enzymes are too high."

"What does all that mean?"

Her dad answered. How had Tessa not noticed how raspy his voice had become? "The doctor said it was an even chance it could be an autoimmune disorder, an infection, or cancer."

All Tessa heard was the last word. She steadied herself on the doorframe. "Cancer?"

"But maybe not," her mom said. "I think he picked up some kind of bacteria from that stupid race. Remember how he lost all the skin on his knees? He started feeling sick less than a week later. Maybe it's Lyme disease or something."

"Doesn't Lyme disease come from a tick?" Tessa asked. "I thought people didn't get Lyme around here."

"It's rare, but it happens," her mom said. "But the doctor said it's weeks before you can be tested for it. Your dad's going to have a CT of his abdomen next week."

Tessa pulled out a chair and slumped into it. She had completely forgotten about the cop, about Ruth, even about how her biological father was a monster. For now, all she could think about was her dad. Her real dad. The one who had done everything a dad could ever do for his daughter for eighteen years.

"I guess we've both been keeping secrets from each other," her dad said. "But, Tessa, we're a family. We should handle this together."

She had been so self-centered, thinking everything revolved around her. Her parents hadn't been ignoring her and Phoebe on purpose. Instead, they had barely been holding it together, trying to protect them. Now they were laying their cards on the table, and she should, too.

"I didn't want to tell you because I was… ashamed, I guess."

"Ashamed?" her dad said. "Why would you ever be ashamed?"

Tessa couldn't keep the tremble out of her voice. "I've had all these big ideas about who my biological parents might be. But none of them was my bio mom being only fifteen when I was born. And when that lady and another cop told me who my bio dad is, that was so much worse. I didn't know what you would think if you knew the truth."

Her dad tilted his head. "Why would that change anything about what we think about you?"

"Because he's evil." Scenes from the documentary flashed through Tessa's mind. "He's caused so much terror and he's ruined so many lives. Not just the victims, but their families and friends. And it's like he takes some kind of twisted delight in it."

"But he doesn't have anything to do with you," her dad said. "With who you really are. He's never even seen you. We've known you for eighteen years, and we know how you are. You're kind. You're caring—"

"And creative," her mom added. "Friendly. Helpful."

"But I'm impatient." Tessa hesitated, then blurted out, "And I get so angry sometimes. What if I got that from him? After all, I've got half his genes."

"Do you really think you'll murder someone?" Her mom blew out a puff of air. "There's no serial-killer gene, Tessa."

"But that's who I come from, and I can never, ever escape it."

Her mom again started to object, but her dad laid his hand on her arm.

In a gruff voice, he said, "It's true you'll never have a different birth father. But values don't come from your genes. That man may have contributed half your DNA—but your mother and I are the ones who raised you, loved you, taught you. But I won't say we made you, because you are making yourself. And we are so proud of the job you are doing."

Maxwell Holloway intones, "It's two years before the Portland Phantom strikes again. This time his chosen victim is Rachel Rule, a runner who regularly competed in marathons and was even sponsored by Nike. But Rachel couldn't outrun the Phantom."

As he speaks, the screen shows a photograph of Rachel, clad in black spandex running briefs and a matching bra top, crossing a finish line, her fists raised in victory.

"When Rachel's body was found, she was still wearing her running clothes. That made the rainbow scarf knotted around her bruised neck stand out even more. The scarf had been hand-knit by Lindsey Turner.

"And as investigators delve into this case,

a disturbing revelation surfaces—Rachel's driver's license is missing." He waggles his eyebrows. "A stolen memento authorities know will become another puzzle piece in the Phantom's twisted game."

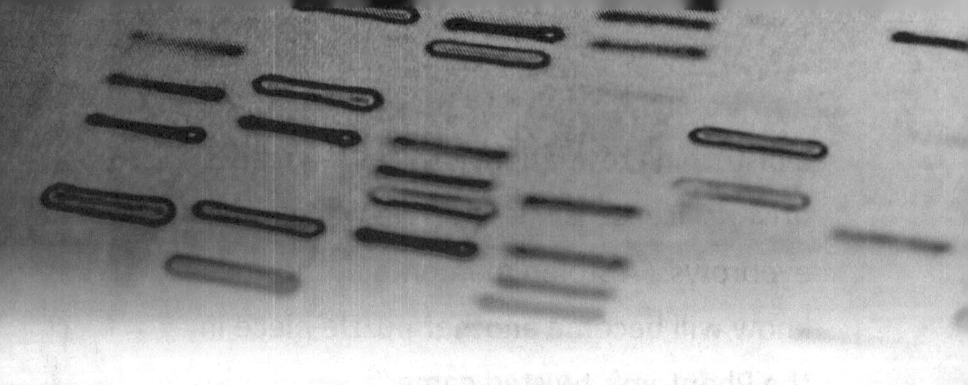

TESSA

Lost

TESSA SHIFTED IN BED, TRYING TO GET COMFORT-able. As if what was keeping her awake was something that could be solved by how she arranged her arms and legs. She had been restless for hours. Sleep felt like an impossibility.

If only she could go back in time. She would tell herself to bury El's gift in the garbage can as soon as she left. Tell herself to stop asking questions. Tell herself that learning the identity of her parents would not make her feel like she finally belonged.

Now, Tessa knew most of the truth and wished she knew none of it. Everything she'd learned had brought her no peace, only pain. Her mother had just been a kid. And her father was a monster. Did that make her half a monster? Or maybe something even worse, because she was the product of two broken people?

Tessa had been acting like a child, telling herself fairy tales. She had gotten what she thought she wanted, realizing too late it was only coal and ashes. Ashes from her mother, who had been far too young to have a baby and then just walked away. Coal from her father, an evil man who had killed a young woman just a few weeks ago.

What would happen when people learned the truth? Even if the police tried to keep it quiet, she was sure someday, somehow, it would leak. There was a whole battalion of armchair detectives out there determined to unmask her biological father's identity. Tessa would just be further grist for their mill.

She switched from lying on her left side to lying on her right. It didn't feel any better.

Plus, the dad who had raised her was sick. Every day for the past eighteen years, he had told her he loved her, not just with words, but with the way he looked at her and how he treated her. But tonight she had seen a different expression on his face. Even though neither her dad nor mom had said it, they must feel betrayed.

Was it even fair of Tessa to consider this her home after all those years of imagining her "real parents" were far better, that if only she were with them, they would be raising her up to her full and true potential?

In her quest to find her true home, had she lost the only one she had ever known?

Tessa pressed her face into her pillowcase and cried.

KEISHA

Similar

THE TASK FORCE HAD REQUESTED THE RECORDS of every male student and staff member who had been at Brookwillow around the time Ruth got pregnant. While the school was cooperating, the information was stored in an old program that hadn't been used for over ten years, and the company that made it had gone out of business.

And while the entries in Ruth's journal would probably have been more than enough to get her punished by her family and her church, the girl had been careful about not naming whoever she had been hooking up with.

Even so, as the task force took their seats around the conference table this morning, there was still a buzz of energy. Learning about Ruth had been the break they had been waiting years for.

At the front of the room, Shane tacked two photos of Ruth to the bulletin board. They had been used for student ID and then the annual and appeared to be the only photos ever taken of her. Jared had told them Reapers did not take personal photographs.

The differences between Ruth's freshman and sophomore photos were striking. In the intervening year, Ruth's eyes had added shadows. Her face had thinned out even as the body hidden by her voluminous dress must have grown. Within a week of sitting for the second photo, she would give birth to her secret daughter and then disappear.

Now, one by one, Shane tacked up photos of the Phantom's known victims under Ruth's photos.

"Maybe they don't exactly look like sisters, but they sure look like cousins." Noah said what everyone was thinking. Like Ruth, they all had upturned noses, high cheekbones, long dark hair.

"So was Ruth the original victim and all these other girls his attempt to re-create the experience?" Sanjay tapped his pen against his lips.

"But if Ruth's dead, where's her body?" Lori countered. "Maybe the victims are just a twisted way of getting back at her for leaving. Look at Ted Bundy. All his victims had long dark hair, parted in the middle. They all looked like the young woman who broke off their engagement. But he never hurt her, just her look-alikes. She lived, and those other girls died."

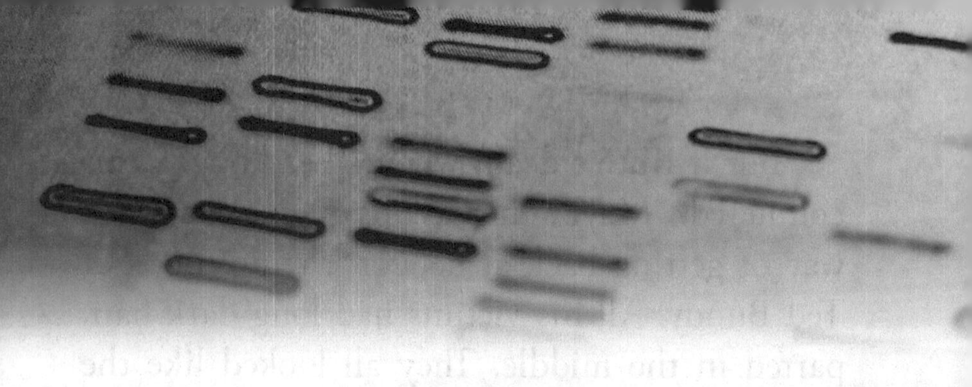

QUENTIN

Justified

QUENTIN WASN'T SLEEPING. THE STRESS OF TRYING to get to know his daughter from afar was getting to him. He needed to calm his nerves, and there was only one good solution.

And luckily, he already had a girl on deck. The one who had originally just been for practice would now be elevated to the real thing. She would be Quentin's latest project.

Wren Phillips, or as he had originally dubbed her, Short Skirt.

Wearing his favorite tan driving gloves, the ones nearly the same color as his skin, Quentin stood in front of her apartment door. He set the gray plastic box about the size of a shoebox next to his feet, then took out his pick set. This was his fifth or sixth time picking this lock, so it should take only a few seconds.

After setting the tensioner, he rapidly wiggled his favorite pick up and down, a motion some lock pickers likened to teeth brushing, then raked it back and forth, and finally moved it in a circle. One by one, he felt the pins retract. A second later, he was slipping inside Short Skirt's sad studio apartment. It was furnished with a twin bed, a rickety card table, a folding chair, and a purple beanbag chair with patches of matted fur. As usual, the bed was unmade, a pile of dirty laundry next to it.

He knew every inch of the small space from the other times he had rifled through her belongings, taking nothing and noting everything. He knew where she kept the knives, the scissors, her hair spray, and even the cast-iron frying pan. Wren didn't own a gun. If she had, he might have removed the bullets. It could be fun to play with your food, like a cat letting a mouse think it was escaping before pouncing again. Twice he had enjoyed watching a project's face when the hammer of their gun clicked and nothing happened.

The card table that was both Wren's dining room table and study area was covered with papers and dirty dishes. More dishes were piled on the counter and in the kitchen sink. Quentin winced in disgust. She was lucky she didn't have roaches.

Wren would be back at 6:40. He knew her schedule as well as he knew his own or her neighbors', neither one of whom was home right now. He set the box in the corner.

Then he waited, bouncing a little on his toes. His breathing was fast, his pulse audible in his ears. Inside his gloves, he could feel sweat gathering on his palms. To quiet his heart, Quentin practiced his box breathing. In for four counts, hold for four, out for four counts, hold for four.

At the sound of Wren's key in the lock, he felt the hot wash of adrenaline. As she stepped inside, he slipped behind her and put his hand over her mouth while kicking the door closed.

Sometimes this was the point when they tried to fight. But not Wren. She was rigid with shock and fear, but she didn't try to mule kick him, didn't try to turn her keys into a weapon, didn't try to bite his hand or squirm out of his grasp.

"Sh, sh, sh," he whispered into the white shell

of her ear. She smelled like coconut shampoo and clove cigarettes. "If you do everything I say, I'll let you go." He waited until she stilled. "Do you understand?"

Under his hand, her head bobbed. "I'm on the run from the police. All I need is some food, maybe some money, and then I'll be on my way." In his experience, this lie worked the best. People wanted to believe. Wanted more than anything to believe they could live.

Some men like him controlled their victims with a gun or a knife or a flurry of blows. Quentin relied on his words and his wits. It might be a risk, but it was also a much greater thrill.

"So will you be quiet?" he asked. She nodded again and he dropped his hand. Wren stepped back and turned to face him.

Quentin had entered the state of hyperawareness that made him realize how most of the time the world was dim and muffled. Both the girl and her sad, sorry apartment looked hyperrealistic. He saw the pores on her nose, the spots in her irises, every crumb on the table behind her.

"I don't want to hurt you," he said quietly. "I just want to get as far away as possible."

She started to move and he stiffened. But she just leaned down and picked her key ring off the floor. She held it out. "Take my car. Just take it. I won't call the police." She blinked and a tear ran down her face.

He reached out, keeping his movements slow and steady so she didn't flinch. But instead of taking the keys, he ran the knuckle of his glove down the silvery track of her tear.

Now all he could see was her. Everything else disappeared. The way she was panting, her shoulders moving with little jerks. Her long hair. Her slightly crooked front teeth. Her wide eyes. And her slender neck.

Her neck, her neck, her neck.

And suddenly his hands were around it. Watching her pupils widen, her hair fly out as she struggled, her hands pull ineffectually at his wrists after she dropped the keys.

And then her face was replaced by Ruth's, the way it always was. But today it wasn't the face she had had at fifteen. Today Quentin imagined the thirty-three-year-old Ruth. The Ruth who might have been.

He killed her anyway.

And when he was finished, he took a deep, relaxing breath and then gently lowered her to the floor. His muscles were warm and relaxed, and his mind was pleasantly blank. Earlier, his nose had been stuffy from seasonal allergies, but now he could breathe freely.

Wren looked graceless, boneless. He wasn't one of those who posed his victims, tied a bow around their neck or left them in an embarrassing position. But he did like to neaten things up. He looked around. The bed was out. Too many connotations. Should he sit her up against a wall? Then he decided the best place to leave her was the beanbag chair.

With a grunt, he bent over and hoisted her onto his shoulder. "Dead weight" was more than just a saying. The girl was still warm, but loose in a way even an unconscious person wasn't. Something poked his neck, but he barely registered it through the adrenaline still jolting in his veins.

After nestling her in the purple plush, he brushed the hair back from her face and closed her eyes with a soft press of his gloved fingertips. Then he straightened her clothing. As he did, he saw what had poked him. Fastened to her sweater was that pin she had been so proud of making, sterling silver in the shape of a spiral. He undid it and pulled it free, then moved under the light to make sure there was no blood on the point.

The silver gleamed. Quentin set it aside for later. Then he methodically took what he wanted. He left the cash and credit cards, the expensive headphones, her laptop and phone. Instead, he pocketed a half dozen small keepsakes he had noted on earlier visits: an antique locket, a tattered concert ticket stub, a water-damaged Polaroid of a black-and-white cat, and a chipped porcelain rabbit no bigger than his thumb.

Once he was satisfied, he swabbed her fingers with an alcohol wipe and cleaned under her nails with her own file. Afterward, he washed it and put it back in her bathroom drawer.

He opened the gray plastic box. Inside was a small silver battery-operated vacuum about the size and shape of a thermos. He snapped on the black hose, then hummed under his breath as he ran the nozzle over her neck and then lightly over her clothes. He didn't think he had left any DNA, but better safe than sorry.

When he was finished, he put the vacuum

back in its box. He would dump its contents in a public garbage can near the Goodwill donation bin. Before closing the box, he added his new souvenirs and took out the item he had brought with him: a photo of a preteen Alida next to her mother, smiling in front of a Christmas tree. He propped it under Wren's chin.

Hoping it would make it more difficult for the medical examiner to determine the time she died, Quentin cranked up the thermostat.

Before he left, he took a glass from the cupboard. He held it up to the light to make sure it was clean, then ran water from the tap and drank it. As he tipped the glass back, his eyes were on his handiwork. Would her mother now feel justified in her warnings?

After he swallowed the last of the water, he ran the green sponge he found in the sink around the glass, rinsed it out, dried it, and put it back in the cupboard.

Dennis Rader, known as BTK, had done that, and Quentin thought it was a nice touch.

KEISHA

Hunting

AT 5:17 FRIDAY MORNING, KEISHA WAS AWAKENED by a task force group text, telling them to come in ASAP. She made it before six, but many were already there, buzzing with curiosity.

A few minutes later, Shane hurried into the room and everyone hushed.

"A young woman was murdered near Bridgetown University last night. Wren Phillips. Strangled. And this photo was found on her chest." He held up a clear plastic evidence bag.

Even from a distance, Keisha recognized the subjects. Alida and her mom. The Phantom had struck again. A bolt of adrenaline shot from her head to her heels.

"This is not like him." Lori's brow furrowed. "Usually he goes years between kills. Why kill again so soon?"

"To taunt us?" Sanjay suggested. "To show he's more powerful than we are?"

"We put a rush on the autopsy," Shane said. "We have only preliminary results and none of the lab work, but she was definitely strangled. Doc thinks the sex-assault kit will be negative, as usual. He didn't see anything under her nails, but the fingernail cuttings and fingertip swabs are still being processed. Same with her clothing."

Keisha knew that if possible, rather than cutting off the victim's clothes, they would have undressed her like a giant doll. Every item of the deceased's would now have outsize meaning to her family, even the last clothes she had worn. An examiner would use an alternative light source to identify any stains that could not be seen by human eyes.

"Is she a student at Bridgetown?" Lisa asked. "Like Betty and Candy?"

"She was," Shane said. "That could just be a coincidence, given over half the student body is made up of the type of women he targets."

The task force dispersed to learn as much about Wren Phillips as fast as possible. Keisha interviewed several people in Wren's apartment building, but no one knew her more than to smile at, and no one had heard or seen anything suspicious.

In the early afternoon, Shane summoned them back. Examiners had found a tiny spot of fresh blood on Wren's sweater. In DNA's infancy, a blood-stain needed to be the size of a quarter for there to be enough to test. Now the necessary amount was so small it was almost invisible to the eye.

Shane said, "Wren's best friend mentioned she always wore this big spiral sterling silver pin she made." He patted his chest. "Right here. Right where they found the blood. But the pin's not on the body and it's not in the apartment."

Noah said what they were all thinking. "It sounds like just the kind of thing he likes to take as a souvenir."

The next morning, the task force was summoned back. Shane had asked the lab to rush the DNA results, and they were now in. The room fell silent as soon as he entered.

"The blood was male," he said. "No surprise there." He took a deep breath. "The thing is, it doesn't match the Phantom. At least, it's not a match to the skin cells we found under Candy Rossner's fingernails."

The room filled with questions and expressions of disbelief. Shane held up his hand to quiet them.

"Could it be a copycat killer?" Lori asked.

"That's very unlikely. The killer deliberately displayed the photo of Alida and her mother on Wren's body. That's the same type of thing the Phantom has done for every one of his kills after Dana. And while it's possible someone managed to create this photo—according to Alida's mother, she has the same photo at home—it has never been released to the public."

"So how is it possible the DNA doesn't match?" Noah sounded exhausted.

Shane tilted his head. "It's possible another altercation happened prior to Candy being murdered. According to her dorm mate, Candy had a drinking problem and could be aggressive when she overindulged."

Lisa said what Keisha was thinking. "But Candy scratching someone had to have happened that day, or the DNA wouldn't have been recoverable. Is it really possible she fought with one guy and then a different one came along and murdered her?"

"I'm actually thinking we could be looking at two killers working together."

The room was silent as the task members absorbed this. Two serial killers wasn't unheard of. Cousins, friends, roommates. Sometimes even lovers.

Shane grinned, and it was somehow feral. "But I saved the good news for last. The guy who left the blood is in CODIS." CODIS was a national criminal DNA database, run by the FBI, that allowed state and local crime labs to share and compare DNA profiles. "We're getting an arrest warrant now. We're going to get him."

"Why are we so fascinated by serial killers?" Maxwell Holloway's thick eyebrows rise.

"The serial killer is like a fun house mirror held up to society." Raising her flat hand in front of her face, Dr. Evelyn Thornfield tilts her head from one side to the other, miming looking in a mirror. "When we examine the serial killer, we actually see many characteristics our society values, like drive, persistence, and fortitude. This blurs the boundary between good and evil. In fact, ordinary people and serial killers have many of the same traits. We daydream about power, we idealize ourselves, we deceive ourselves, and we indulge in secret behaviors we don't want others to know about."

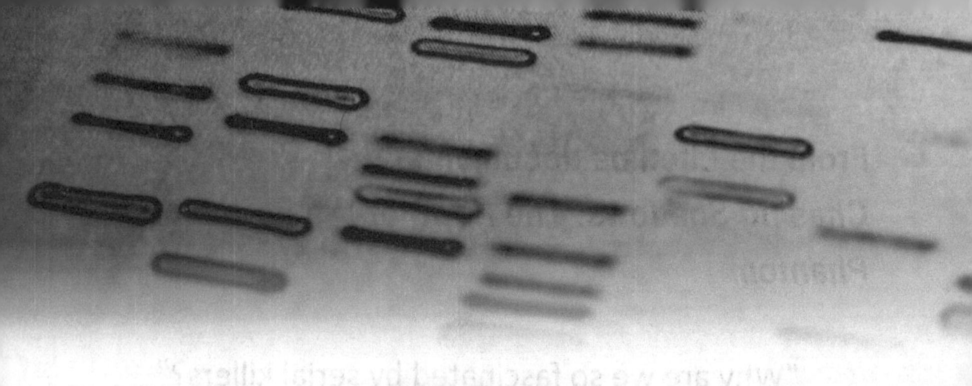

KEISHA

Mix-up

THE VIEWING ROOM WAS PACKED, NOT JUST WITH the task force, but also with any cop or unsworn employee who could squeeze in to watch the Phantom be questioned through a one-way mirror. He had been arrested only a few hours after his blood had been found on the latest victim.

When Shane and Noah led in Frank Porter, Keisha's first thought was he didn't look like a killer. But then again, someone who looked like a killer would have been caught by now. Frank, who worked as a bike shop mechanic, was about six feet tall and wiry, with a shaved head. He wore jeans, a maroon polo, and work boots.

Keisha did the math. He was in his mid-fifties,

which meant he must have started his second career as a serial killer at nearly forty. Maybe there were other victims they didn't know about.

The three sat at the table, with Frank on one side and the two cops on the other. Shane set several fat files between them.

It was an old police trick. Make the suspect think the evidence against him was overwhelming, even if the pages inside the folders were blank. In this case, it wasn't even a ruse. They had reams of information about the Phantom. But the only evidence they had linking Frank and the Phantom was the single drop of blood on Wren's sweater. Frank's blood. While he had been arrested thirty years ago, he had stayed out of trouble since. At least on paper.

For the recording, Shane stated the date, time, and the people in the room, then he rattled off Frank's Miranda rights. "Do you understand these rights, which I have explained to you?"

"Yeah," Frank muttered.

Shane said, "Okay, having these rights in mind, are you willing to speak with us?"

"Yeah, I'll talk to you. I don't have anything to hide."

"We're here today to talk about the death of Wren Phillips."

Keisha noticed Shane didn't say murder. For this moment, in this room, death would be portrayed as simply a thing that had happened to Wren. It might have been natural, it might have been an accident. It didn't have to be Frank's fault.

"Dude, I don't know her."

Noah pulled the top file closer, found a photo of Wren, and slid it over.

Frank regarded it without touching it. Keisha made a mental note. If she had been doing the questioning, she would have handed it to him. Forced him to interact with it.

He raised his head. "I've never seen her before."

Shane said, "Maybe she brought in her bike to be fixed and you talked to her?"

The problem with this, Keisha knew, was Wren did not appear to own a bike. There wasn't one in her studio apartment, and none of the bikes in the building's bike area seemed to belong to her. Her friends said they didn't remember her having one.

"No." Frank crossed his arms.

As for Frank himself, his main transportation was a bike. It could explain why he had never dumped the bodies of the victims in a more remote area. And the idea of a bike as a getaway vehicle was interesting. A bike was basically invisible. No one noticed the make and model of a bike. You could come and go without attracting notice. You could even go places cars couldn't.

"Maybe you met her in a bar?" Shane asked.

"I don't drink. I go to a lot of NA and AA meetings." Narcotics Anonymous and Alcoholics Anonymous. "I keep my nose clean."

Noah said, "This girl lives only a mile and a half from you. Sure you haven't seen her at Freddie's or something?" Fred Meyer, or Freddie's, was the regional grocery chain.

Frank's gaze was fixed somewhere just past Shane. "I'm guessing thousands of people live a mile and a half from her."

"But nobody else left their DNA on her." Noah leaned forward and stabbed his finger in Frank's face. "Your blood was on her sweater. So don't tell us you don't know her."

"But I don't. I'm telling you, I've never seen that girl before in my life."

"You've been in trouble before, right, Frank?" Shane's voice was soft. "That's why your DNA was in the system."

"Just once." He pinched the bridge of his nose. "But it messed me up forever."

"Tell me what happened."

"I played baseball in college. Then I tore my rotator cuff. The team doc prescribed these heavy-duty painkillers so I could keep pitching." Frank's mouth twisted. "When the season was over, he wouldn't prescribe any more. But the pain was still there. I started buying drugs on the street and burning through money. One day I decided to rob a 7-Eleven with an Airsoft gun. I spent nine months in jail. And I've been clean ever since." His exhale was loud enough the microphone picked it up. "Do you know how hard it is to get a job when you have a record? I was just lucky my boss took a chance on me. But I can never get those years back. All my high school buddies have wives and kids. Some have grandkids. I don't even have a girlfriend." He flinched as if belatedly realizing this might sound bad. "But that's not a reason for me to go around killing women."

"That must be frustrating." Shane managed to sound truly sympathetic. "And I am sure there is a reason that what happened, happened. Maybe this girl invited you home and then changed her mind. Maybe she had a weapon or tried to fight with you, something of that nature. I don't know what the reason was. But that's why we're here. There are always two sides to every story. I just want to hear your side."

Frank sat back and crossed his arms tightly. "But I don't have a side. I didn't have anything to do with this. Look, I feel bad for her and everything, but I didn't do anything to her." He stressed his next words. "Because I've never met her."

Shane grimaced. "Frank, Frank, Frank. It is not a matter of whether you did or didn't do it. Because we've got your blood on her sweater."

Frank shook his head. "But that has to be a lie. Or a mistake. A mix-up at the lab."

"DNA doesn't lie. And I think it would be nice to get what happened off your shoulders, because I'm sure it's been bothering you."

Noah leaned forward. "Did she turn on you? That wouldn't surprise me one bit, the things I've heard about her." Noah was playing bad cop, not just in regard to Frank, but also in regard to the victim. In their search for the truth, cops were allowed to lie. "We're hearing that girl had a real temper. But if you don't get your story told, it's going to look bad for you."

"There is no story." Frank ran his palm over his shaved head. Did he shave it because he was balding or in the hope of leaving as little DNA as possible?

Noah slipped in the next question. "So tell us about your friend, Frank. The one you do this with. It was probably his idea, right?"

Keisha knew they were already looking at Frank's friends, relatives, coworkers, neighbors. Even people incarcerated at the same time he had been, since people in jail learned from one another. But it would be a lot easier if Frank simply gave them a name.

Noah pushed a little harder. "Did you ever think maybe this guy was just setting you up? Letting you take the fall so he can walk away scot-free?"

Frank's face scrunched up. "What are you talking about? What friend? I don't know this girl, I didn't kill her, and I don't know who you're talking about."

"Look," Shane said. "We know you were there. Maybe you were there and you watched this guy do something bad and there was nothing you could do to stop it. But now you can. You can tell us his name. And if you're afraid of him, I promise we can keep you safe."

Frank rubbed his eyes. "I was never there, and I don't know who did it."

"The thing is," Shane said, "we know you were there. And we know the man people call the Portland Phantom was there. So we need you to tell us who he is."

Like everyone else, Keisha was watching Frank's face.

Frank Porter didn't look resigned.

He didn't look angry.

He looked confused.

QUENTIN

Monster

A TINY SPOT OF FRESH BLOOD HAD BEEN FOUND ON Wren Phillips's sweater, blood Quentin had missed after her handmade pin jabbed him.

Only the blood hadn't matched him, but instead Frank Porter, a guy who had been added to CODIS after a single botched robbery decades ago.

So how was that possible? Quentin did a little digging.

Bad blood. That's what his father had said Quentin had. The leukemia had made the developing blood cells in his bone marrow multiply out of control to the point they crowded out his healthy blood cells, leaving Quentin near death.

Finally, the doctors had destroyed his defective bone marrow and replaced it with a healthy donor's. Immediately, the new bone marrow had started doing its job, making healthy blood. The blood that now ran in the veins of two people: Quentin and Frank Porter. So when Quentin had left blood evidence behind, it appeared to be Porter's.

The rest of Quentin—his skin, organs, and hair—was still made up of his original DNA. The bone marrow transplant had left him a human chimera, a Greek word that had originally meant a fire-breathing monster made up of a goat, a snake, and a lion.

A fire-breathing monster. Quentin liked the sound of that.

BREAKTHROUGH IN PORTLAND PHANTOM CASE: MAN ARRESTED AFTER DECADES-LONG HUNT

By Megan Callahan, *The Oregonian*

PORTLAND—In a stunning development in one of the nation's most chilling unsolved serial-killer cases, police have announced the arrest of 55-year-old Frank Porter in connection with the murder of a woman believed to be the ninth victim of the elusive Portland Phantom. A drop of fresh blood found on 21-year-old Wren Phillips's clothing after her murder last week proved to be a DNA match to Porter, who previously served time for aggravated robbery. But while the arrest is a major development in the case, detectives say it may not represent the end.

Unknown male DNA was also recovered 13 years ago, this time from under the fingernails of the Phantom's second victim,

21-year-old Candy Rossner. That DNA has long been considered the key to identifying the Phantom. But the recovered DNA from Wren Phillips—an exact match for Porter—does not match the DNA found on Rossner.

For years, the Phantom's killings have followed a grim pattern: one victim every two to three years, all in their twenties or early thirties, all female-identifying, all strangled.

"Wren Phillips was killed in the exact same way as the other victims," said Detective Shane Morrison, lead investigator on the Portland Phantom Task Force. "Strangled, no signs of sexual assault, and with, most notably, an item belonging to Alida Cleary, the previous victim, found on her body. That's the Phantom's signature."

But even with that signature, Phillips's death represents a significant departure from the previous killings. Cleary was murdered Sept. 1, but then just six weeks later, the Phantom struck again, killing Phillips. This sudden acceleration—along with the unexpected

DNA match to Porter—has forced investigators to consider new possibilities, including a theory the Phantom may not be working alone, or that the long-standing original DNA evidence may not have come from Rossner's killer after all.

One possibility being strongly considered is that Porter is an accomplice or apprentice of the original Phantom. "We're combing through Porter's past, especially his time in jail," Morrison said. "Whether one person or two is responsible for the Phantom's murders—or whether we've been looking for the wrong DNA all along—is something we're working to unravel. We've always believed this case would eventually come down to the smallest pieces of evidence. Now we're reexamining every one of them."

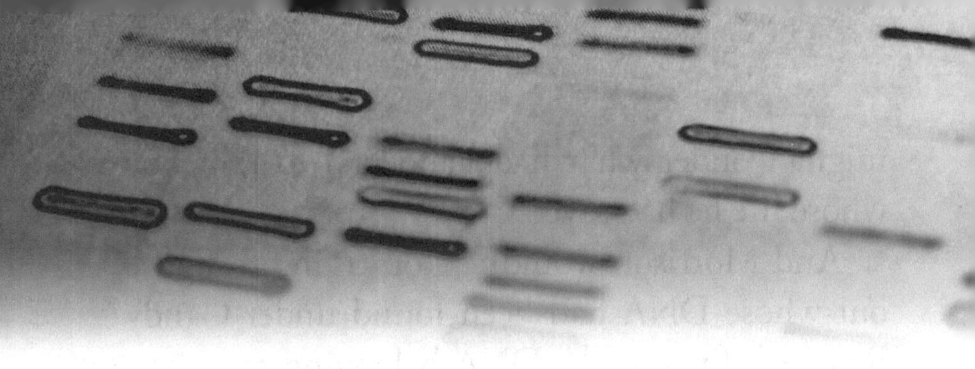

QUENTIN

Limits

FOR QUENTIN, THE WORLD WAS BOTH CONTRACT-ing and expanding.

Contracting as the police circled the truth. Many times, Quentin had watched Shane Morrison being interviewed on TV. He knew the detective wouldn't rest until he got the puzzle pieces to fit exactly. The cops would keep interrogating Frank Porter, tracing him back through time, mapping his whereabouts, questioning everyone he knew, but they would never be able to square him with the killings.

Porter might even eventually remember his frat holding a bone marrow drive, and how he had been a perfect match for a five-year-old. He might wonder what had happened to that boy whose life he had saved.

And Morrison wouldn't stop trying to figure out whose DNA had been found under Candy Rossner's fingernails, DNA belonging to a man they knew had fathered Tessa. Tanner had said they were looking at Brookwillow staff as well as students. Even though Quentin had actually been employed by the local police department, eventually someone might figure it out.

Besides, why should Frank Porter get all the credit for Quentin's hard work?

Quentin's world was also expanding as he obsessed over his newfound daughter.

It wasn't enough, though, just to observe Tessa from afar. He wanted to talk to her. Explain to her. Influence her. Maybe even show off a little.

But for him to get close to Tessa, Ruth needed to be alive, or at least seem to be. His daughter was bound to be skittish.

Quentin started with the two existing photos of Ruth, the ones taken when she was at

Brookwillow. Now he needed to age her up. AI made this kind of thing child's play. In less than an hour, he had generated multiple versions of a Ruth who would never be. Finally, he chose one with a half smile and a direct gaze. And while Quentin saw so much of himself in Tessa, he had to admit there was a resemblance between the older "Ruth" and his daughter.

Something about looking at Ruth's eyes in the imaginary photos started feeling strangely real. Like in some alternate reality there was still a Ruth, now in her mid-thirties. All grown up, no longer naive and sheltered. Would he still find her so irresistible?

He created an account for the imaginary Ruth with only her first name, not even a bio. Just Ruth and the new photo. Unlike his other sock puppet accounts, he didn't follow anyone or attempt to get anyone to follow him. Instead, he sent a message request to Tessa's profile.

"Now that you're eighteen, I had to join this site so I could say hi. I just wanted to see how you turned out."

Two days went by. With every passing hour, Quentin grew more anxious. Had she simply deleted the message? Finally, his phone alerted him to a response. He went into his office and locked the door.

"Who are you?" Tessa had written.

He didn't think, just answered. "Who you think I am."

"I've tried to find you and I can't."

"I changed my name when I moved to California," he typed.

"If you're my mom, how come no one has heard from you and no one can find you?"

"There's a reason I've stayed gone all these years. The Reapers would give anything to force me to rejoin their cult." They'd done it before. Ruth had told him about it.

His daughter was no pushover. Now she wrote, "You know that old cartoon that says, 'On the internet, nobody knows you're a dog'? I need you to prove you're really who you say you are."

"Sure," he immediately agreed. "Do you want to have a video call?" As he spoke, he opened a different app and uploaded the supposed current photo of Ruth.

With AI, you could appear to be a politician—or fool one. You could make a famous actor credibly wish someone a happy birthday. You could make your own porn with famous faces and other people's bodies. Kids did it all the time with photos of unsuspecting classmates. You could even talk via video in real time, interacting with someone else.

"Okay, give me your number and I'll call you," Tessa wrote. "But I'm going to block my number until I'm sure who you are."

Like Quentin, his daughter was smart. He liked that.

He gave her a number that autoforwarded to his own, one he could also answer on his computer. There would be a slight lag as his voice was filtered to a higher pitch.

The phone rang and he answered it within the AI. On his screen, he saw Tessa with a smaller inset of "Ruth." That was who she was seeing. Not Quentin, but the mother she might have had.

"Oh my God," she breathed, staring. "It *is* really you."

He knew how Tessa was feeling. He could look at her all he wanted without arousing her suspicion. His eyes drank her in.

"In the flesh," he said, and a millisecond later

"Ruth's" lips said the exact same thing, only in a woman's voice.

It wasn't perfect. In fact, if Tessa looked closely, there would likely be some anomaly—odd shadows, ears that didn't quite match, or unnatural patterns in the AI-generated Ruth's hair.

Tessa shook her head and blinked, as if making herself focus. "What's my father's name?"

Straight to the chase. Quentin liked it. "It doesn't matter. I left that part of my life behind years ago. I didn't even know I was pregnant until I had you."

"The police are going to want to talk to you," Tessa said.

Quentin shook his head, and Ruth did, too. He knew from experimentation he could also raise his eyebrows or nod, and his avatar would as well. He channeled a Ruth who had left her past behind. "I'm sure the statute of limitations is well past. Even though your father was quite a bit older than me, it's not like he took advantage of me. I wanted it as much as he did."

"The police think my biological father might have been the Portland Phantom."

A thrill ran up Quentin's spine. He loved his nickname, loved how he had become a legend. "That's not right. I saw on TV they arrested the guy who did it," he made Ruth say. "And I've never seen that man before in my life. He's definitely *not* your father."

"They think he might have been working with my biological father. When I had my DNA done, I was able to figure out you were my mother. And the police told me my father is the one who left DNA on the Phantom's second victim."

"That can't be right." He tried to make Ruth sound perplexed and overwhelmed. "Your father was good to me." He had been, hadn't he? For a second, Quentin imagined a world where he had let Ruth live. But once the adults around her realized she had given birth, they would have pressured her into revealing his identity. "There's no way he was a killer."

"You really need to talk to the police. I can give you the phone number for one of them. She's pretty nice, for a cop."

"It won't make any difference. I heard he died from a heart attack fifteen years ago. Any answers they go looking for will be dead ends."

Quentin shook his head, and the on-screen Ruth did, too. "And I'm not willing to lose the privacy it took me almost twenty years to build. What if the Reapers find out about me and try to force me back? I'm sorry, but I won't do it."

"If you won't talk to the police, will you at least talk to me?"

Quentin let his gut choose his next words. "Just so you can try to persuade me to talk to the police? No thanks."

"Not only for that." Tessa's gaze was intense. "I've been wondering about you my whole life."

The way to make someone want something was to tell them it was off-limits. Once you couldn't have something, it immediately became more desirable.

"I don't think that's a good idea," he made Ruth say.

"But you're my mother," Tessa insisted, her gaze intense. "I want to meet you."

TESSA

Darkness

TESSA BRACED HERSELF ON THE DASH AS VICTOR'S car jolted over a particularly bad pothole. In this industrial part of town, the roads were more hole than tarmac. A few streetlights cast pools of anemic yellow light that only deepened the shadows between them. The handful of businesses still solvent were all locked up tight, metal shutters pulled down over any potential opening. Other buildings seemed to have been abandoned years ago, with gaping black windows and layers of spray-painted tags.

"Are you sure about this?" El said from the back seat. "This neighborhood seems sketchy."

This was not the first time they'd had this

argument. Tessa's biological father might be dead, but she was not going to miss the chance to meet her biological mother. When Tessa had finally told them she would just take an Uber and go visit Ruth by herself, her friends had insisted on accompanying her. Tessa had been afraid Ruth would say no, but she had agreed.

"Yeah, Tessa," Victor agreed, "if she wants to meet you, I still think it should be at a restaurant or something."

"Do you know how much work it was to persuade her? She's scared to be back in Portland again, in case a Reaper someplace recognizes her. She's coming in for only a day, just long enough to talk to me, pick up the evidence, and take it back to where she lives now."

Ruth had explained that when she first ran away, she'd rented a cheap storage unit on the outskirts of Portland, more than twenty miles from where she grew up. She had even lived there illegally for a few weeks, worried that the Reapers were hunting her, until she got up the courage to take the Greyhound to California. She had kept the space because it held evidence against the Reapers. "I guess it's like an insurance policy in case they try to snatch her off the street." Her mom hadn't gone into details as to what the evidence was, but having watched a few documentaries about cults with El, Tessa could guess—abuse, exploitation, neglect. "Ruth said it's really cheap and no one asked any questions."

"I believe the cheap part," Victor muttered as he swerved to avoid another pothole. A few blocks later, they spotted the unlit sign marking the entrance to SAMMY'S STORAGE SOLUTIONS. Behind a rusted chain-link fence topped with menacing spirals of razor wire, a long, single-storied metal building sprawled across the darkened lot.

Victor nosed to a stop in front of the gate. On her phone, Tessa found the access code Ruth had provided and read it aloud so he could tap it in. With creaks and groans, the long gate moved upward like a drawbridge.

"Better hurry," El advised, tilting her head back. "That thing looks like it's about ready to turn into a guillotine."

They made it to the other side without incident. As they parked, the gate slowly lowered back into place with a shriek of metal.

Victor looked around. "Shouldn't your mom's car be here?" Not only was the lot empty, there was no evidence of another human being within eyeshot.

"Maybe she's running late." Ruth had even been cagey about whether she was flying or driving up from California. Tessa checked her phone again. Nothing. "She told me the unit number." Running her phone flashlight over the nearest roll-up metal door, Tessa read off the peeling number. "One hundred eleven. Hers is one nineteen." She started off, walking deeper into the darkness.

"Wait up," El called out. "Isn't that a light on in one of the units?"

El was right. Near the end of the building, a smudged line of luminance marked the bottom of a not-quite-closed roll-up door. Tessa's heart sped up along with her feet. In a few seconds, she would see her mother, the woman she had dreamed about for as long as she had known about her existence.

By the time she reached the unit, she was almost running, with Victor and El hurrying to keep up. The eight-foot-wide roll-up metal door wasn't quite flush to the ground. A soft line of light on the bottom glinted on an open silver padlock lying next to the bottom edge of the door.

"Ruth?" Tessa called.

No answer.

At the center of the door was a white length of cord ending in a loop. Victor leaned over and hauled it with a grunt. The door rose as high as his thighs before he had to reset.

"Ruth?" Tessa repeated in a louder voice. She crouched, trying to see.

El put a hand on her elbow and tried to pull Tessa back, but she shook her off.

"Mom?"

Victor rolled the door the rest of the way up. At first, all they saw was the back of a canvas wardrobe, a six-foot-wide portable closet, taller than Tessa, made of cream-colored cloth. She went around one corner and heard her friends scramble after her.

The room was lit by only a single weak bulb high above their heads. It revealed a shadowy space, about ten by fifteen feet, that was a stark contrast to the decay and desolation outside.

Everything was neat and organized, with plenty of open space. Against the back wall stood two white display cases.

Standing like an island in the center were a nondescript desk and chair. Lined up on top of the desk were a series of black binders.

Tessa glanced over her shoulder at the front of the closet. It was empty. Its real purpose must be to stop prying eyes from seeing inside.

"Is this like your mom's office or something?" El asked.

If it was, her mom wasn't here. It was clear Tessa, El, and Victor were the only people in this room. Everything was so tidy. But the tidiness was somehow more unsettling than a stack of worn moving boxes would have been. The back of Tessa's neck prickled.

El stepped forward, pulled out a binder, and opened it. At the same time, Victor ran his phone flashlight over the display case on the left. Scattered items too small for Tessa to make out glinted back.

"Oh my God," El said in a hushed voice. "This is a scrapbook. It's all clippings about him. About the Phantom."

The prickling spread down Tessa's spine. She moved next to El, and they both looked at the headlines. PHANTOM STRIKES AGAIN, FEAR SPREADS ACROSS PORTLAND, POLICE BAFFLED.

"Why would your mom want to keep all this?"

"Tessa?" Victor's voice was almost unrecognizable. "I think these . . . these are trophies."

Now that her eyes had adjusted, she could pick out some of the objects on display: a brooch here, a neatly folded scarf there, a photograph next to a charm bracelet. Even more chilling were the small white placards set in front of the objects. They were labeled with what Tessa suddenly knew must be names.

Her thoughts were a jumble. Why would Ruth have this stuff? Had she been lying when she said Tessa's father was dead? Were they working together?

Victor sniffed. "Hey, do you smell that? Like oil or something?" El moved closer to Victor as he bent down in front of one of the bookcases.

From behind her, a hand clamped over Tessa's mouth and nose. At the same time, a strong arm snaked around her shoulders. Her heart somersaulted as adrenaline flooded her system. Despite her struggles, she was dragged back past the portable closet and under the door.

When the hand left her mouth, she gathered breath to scream. But by the time she did, the door was already rattling down. The man's other arm moved from her shoulders to around her neck. It tightened, yanking her off-balance as he bent over. She heard a *click*. Tessa knew it was the lock snapping into place.

Inside, El and Victor were yelling her name as they pounded on the door.

"Hello, Tessa," a man's voice said.

She nearly choked on her own breath. His voice was so familiar.

Even if she had never heard it before.

"I'm sorry about this." His fist crashed into her temple. The whole world went dark.

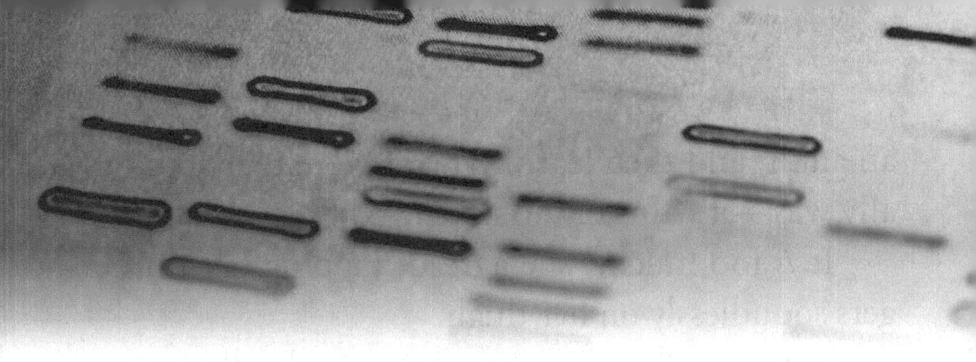

KEISHA

Digging

"IT'S JUST BEEN A LOT TO THINK ABOUT," JARED said on the other end of the line.

"I know." Keisha nodded even though Jared couldn't see her, hoping her impatience wasn't obvious. He had called, saying he had something to tell her, but he still hadn't gotten to the point. As soon as she was done talking to him, she could go back to trying to connect the dots between Frank Porter and the victims.

Jared was still listing everything that had happened. "Finding out Ruth somehow got pregnant and had a baby without anyone knowing, and then meeting that baby, only now she's basically an adult, and then learning who her father actually was—it's almost too much."

"It *is* too much," she agreed, tapping her fingers soundlessly on her thigh.

"Plus, the fact that you guys, with all your resources, can't find Ruth either. For years, I've been making excuses for why she's never been in touch. I told myself she wanted to forget everything and leave it all in the past. Now, I have to admit she's probably dead. Because if Tessa's father was the Phantom, or one half of the Phantom . . ." His voice trailed off.

In Keisha's mind, there was a 99.9 percent chance Ruth was dead. Murdered. Probably not long after she gave birth. Either at the hands of the Phantom or whomever she had trusted to help her escape. Possibly even one of her parents, if they had freaked out about their young, unmarried daughter having a baby.

"The thing is, the day she left? I thought I saw her. Saw Ruth."

"What?" He had Keisha's full attention now. "Where?"

"It was just before school let out. I was in class,

looking out the window, when I saw her coming in a side door."

"Are you sure it was her?"

"I didn't see her face, but no one else at school wore dresses like that. I thought she was feeling better and had come to pick up her homework assignments. School was important to her."

"So you didn't talk to her?"

"No. And I didn't see her either. Later, when we realized she'd run away, I figured she might have come to school to say goodbye to me. And then chickened out or gotten worried I'd tell our parents and they would prune her back." He took a deep, shaky breath. "But what if school was the last place she was? Ever? What if she came there to talk to the guy who was Tessa's father and never left? After all, the only place she could have met that guy was at school."

"We still haven't ruled out everyone from the church." But they had done their best, dealing with high-up Reapers who smiled and agreed to help and then did as little as possible. To a man (and they were all men), they had been adamant no Reaper could have done that to a girl.

But then again, BTK had been president of his church's council.

Jared's voice sped up. "So if Ruth didn't come to school to get her homework or to tell me good-bye, she must have come to talk to whoever was the father. To tell him about the baby."

"It's possible," Keisha said. "Maybe more than possible."

He was silent for so long she wondered if they had been disconnected.

"Jared?"

"The thing is, they were building a new stadium at the time. The ground was all torn up. I think they poured the concrete the next week-end. My boyfriend likes to watch true crime shows. People are always doing that, burying their victims and then covering up the grave with concrete. Claiming it's a patio or whatever."

A chill went through her. "We'll check into it. I'll let you know what we find."

As soon as she hung up, Keisha messaged Shane, asking about having ground-penetrating radar used on the stadium. Utility companies and archeologists had used GPR for decades to find buried pipes and cables, but sometimes it came in handy for law enforcement. It used high-frequency pulses that went into the ground and were then reflected back to the surface. A special software took variations in the elapsed time and made a visual representation of what was under the earth. So while GPR couldn't exactly find bodies, it could find "anomalies," even roughly estimate their size.

In other words, it could give you a place to start digging.

QUENTIN

Legend

"TESSA," QUENTIN SAID SOFTLY.

He was sitting in the red chair Santa's butt occupied four weeks a year. The other forty-eight weeks the chair was kept in this basement storage area with the rest of the university's Christmas decorations. No one would be down here until the day after Thanksgiving, and whatever was going to happen next would be over by then.

Slowly, his daughter opened her eyes. She blinked, and then her lids closed again, her chin nodding back to her chest.

Maybe she thought she was dreaming. They were surrounded by a bizarre winter wonderland. Giant Styrofoam snowmen. Wire reindeer as big as horses. Plastic candy canes the size of telephone poles. Quentin was flanked by toy soldiers larger than he was, arms stiff by their sides, their smiles painted lines.

After propping an unconscious Tessa in a red wicker sleigh, Quentin had spent the last ten minutes examining her features. The arch of her eyebrows. The set of her eyes. Both were familiar. He saw them in his bathroom mirror every day. Her pointed chin, he thought, came from Ruth, but those high cheekbones were definitely his. Feature by feature, he divided the girl between the two of them. But it wasn't fifty-fifty. It was clear to Quentin that his genes had been far stronger.

"Tessa," he repeated, more insistently. Earlier, he had thought her name sounded like a whisper. Now, he realized it also resembled the hiss of a snake.

Her eyes opened again. She startled and tried to push herself up, then realized her hands were cuffed behind her.

He waited for her to demand to know who he was and where she was, but instead Tessa said, "Where are Victor and El? What did you do to them?"

What he had done was set up a cell phone jammer in the storage space. He had bought it on the dark web months earlier, knowing it would come in handy. After he and Tessa had arranged a time to meet, he had taken two unfiltered cigarettes and rubber banded a dozen wooden matches to the butt end of each. He'd had to buy an imported brand, since all American ones now extinguished themselves if someone wasn't sucking on them every few seconds. Like banning cell phone jammers, it was just another example of today's namby-pambyism. Drunk smokers deserved a fiery end if they fell asleep smoking in bed.

He had guessed she wouldn't come alone. Those troublemaking friends of hers, always sticking their noses in. When Quentin saw from the tracker he'd put on the boy's car that they were nearly there, he had lit the cigarettes, then laid them on top of gasoline-soaked rags under each display cabinet. The cigarettes functioned as improvised timers, giving him about fifteen minutes until they burned down to the matches, which would, in turn, ignite the rags. Then he had hidden nearby, watching. Waiting for the chance to grab his daughter and then lock her loser friends inside.

"Your friends are dead," he said now, not bothering to sugarcoat it.

"What?" Her eyes went wide. "Why?"

"You don't need them. They weren't good for you, anyway."

The corners of Tessa's mouth pulled down. Her shoulders hitched as she swallowed back a sob. Then she wiped all expression from her face. Good. Letting other people know your emotions made you vulnerable. Still, Tessa was a woman. And women were weak.

"That girl was ridiculous, changing the color of her hair as often as she changed her clothes. And I saw how that boy looked at you. I know how boys think."

"You *are* really him," Tessa said. It wasn't a question. "You're the Portland Phantom."

"Quentin Sinclair, at your service." He lifted his shoulders to his ears, smiled, then let his shoulders and the smile drop. "And I think you should call me Dad." Her acknowledgment he was the Phantom made him feel proud. And soon the whole world would know his real name.

"Why did you do it?" Her dark brows drew together. "Why did you kill all those women?"

"Not many people are capable of doing what I did, you know." He tilted his head and regarded her. She was strong and smart, like him. And not overly emotional.

She persisted. "But why did you pick *those* women to kill?"

"They thought they could get away with breaking the rules. Flaunting their bodies. Arguing with their superiors. Selling themselves. Forgetting women were made for men, not other women. Denying God's plan."

It was an icy thrill to explain it all.

Quentin stood and pulled something from his pocket. She shrank back.

"Relax. It's just a necklace your mom used to wear when she was your age. She wants you to have it." It was a fine gold chain with a cross. When he snapped it closed, the hair was standing up on the nape of Tessa's neck. He remembered unfastening it from Ruth's limp body.

"I didn't think I could be a father," he explained. "I didn't believe Ruth when she told me. Of course, I've apologized to her."

Everything was coming full circle, Quentin realized. He would go back to the beginning. But on his own terms. A weaker man, a lesser man, might simply have killed himself before the police came knocking at his door. Or killed Tessa and then himself. Prove he was the one who controlled death, even his own. Show that he was unbreakable, and that no one—including his own flesh and blood—could escape his power.

But why end everything in secret? He would go out with a bang, not a whimper. He would take control of both his and his daughter's legacy in a final act so grand no one would be able to look away. He would be immortalized in books, TV shows, and movies. They would talk about him forever.

Quentin would be a legend.

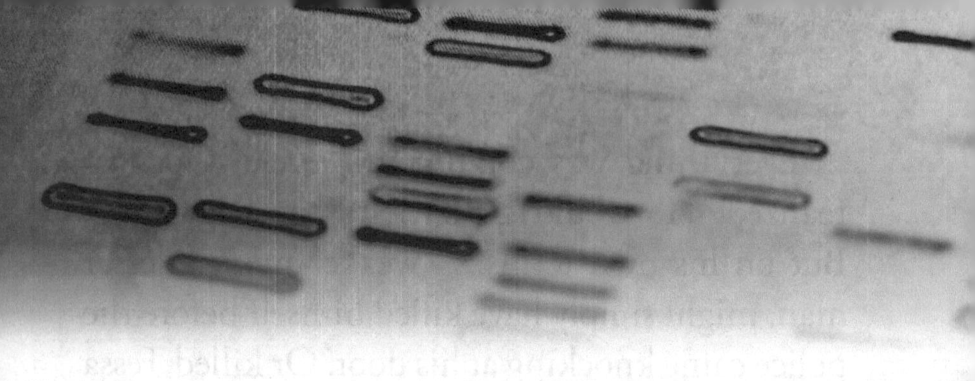

TESSA

Just Like Me

"YOU DON'T GET IT, DO YOU?" TESSA'S BIOLOGICAL father shook his head theatrically. In the low light, his eyes gleamed. "You think you're nothing like me. That you can just walk away from your birthright. But you're not different. I've been watching you long enough to know you're just like me."

Victor and El were dead. Nine women had been strangled to death. And the man who'd killed them all was sure he was better than everyone else.

The features of his face were familiar. Tessa saw a variation of them in the mirror every day. He was letting her peek behind the curtain. Because he thought of her as his.

Only he was nothing like the man she now clearly saw was her real father, the man who had done all the work of raising her. This man wasn't her father. This man, this Quentin Sinclair, knew nothing about Tessa, but he was happy to make pronouncements all the same.

"You know who I am. You know what I've done." Sinclair stepped back and studied her face for any hint of reaction. "You need to understand. It's *in your blood*. I can tell. The same fire I have. The same hunger. You'll see it one day. It might take time, but it's there."

Did he view Tessa as a poor copy of himself, off-center and out of focus? Was she only valuable because she contained a few bits of him that one day might grow stronger?

Tessa knew if she were anyone else, she would already be dead. All her earlier worries she had inherited his evil nature had evaporated. She could never be like this man. Never.

When Sinclair paused for breath, she rushed to wedge in some words of her own.

"So did you ask my mom to contact me?" Her voice quavered, and Tessa let it, even magnified it. She could grieve for El and Victor later. If she survived. Tessa kept remembering her mother's face when they had talked, how Ruth had played hard to get, knowing Tessa would chase after her. "Where is she?"

"Would you like to meet her?" He smiled, and even given everything she knew, it looked sincere. "I can take you to her. She's only twenty minutes away. She's waiting for you."

Longing surged through her. Right now, Tessa needed a mom so badly. But whom she pictured was the mother who had raised her. Ruth, on the other hand, had led her here. Her biological mother was just as evil as this man.

Quentin pulled a phone from his pants pocket. It was Tessa's. He held it in front of her face, and it unlocked. He rapidly tapped his thumbs on the bottom. Then he turned the screen toward her.

He'd texted Phoebe. Her little sister, who was so proud that this school year her parents had allowed her to have a phone.

"Meet me outside. Don't tell Mom or Dad."

"No. Leave her out of this!" The last words were nearly a scream. He didn't flinch. Wherever this strange storage room filled with off-season decorations was located, Tessa could make as much noise as she wanted, and no one would hear.

He shrugged. "That girl isn't blood. She's nothing. Any attention and time she got belonged to you. But you still have some sort of paradoxical connection to her, so I can use her to make sure you'll do as you're told." He grabbed her upper arm. "Now we're going out to my car. You can either go with me or I'll knock you out again and carry you."

"I'll walk." Tessa couldn't help anyone if she was unconscious. Her mind ran in circles as he marched her forward, his hand wrapped around her handcuff chain. How could she stop him from taking Phoebe? How could she save herself? And what horrible thing was he planning?

He opened the door. In an otherwise empty underground parking lot sat an oversize white SUV with black-tinted windows and *Campus Security* emblazoned on the side in blue.

She saw his black clothes in a different light. They were a uniform. His day job was playacting being one of the good guys. How many young women had seen a badge, a name tag, an official vehicle—and trusted a wolf in sheep's clothing?

Sinclair opened the rear door and motioned with his chin for Tessa to sit. When she did, her cuffed hands fit into a molded recess. A metal grate separated her from the front seat, and there were no interior handles on the doors. The only way she could leave would be for him to let her out. He got in, drove up and out of the lot, and started toward her house. Outside, she could see other cars, but no one would be able to see her through the tinted windows. Could she scream when he opened the door? Would that be enough to make Phoebe run back inside?

After parking outside her house, he turned and held up a gun. It was black and plain, a simple machine meant for one thing only: killing. "Not one peep, or Phoebe dies. Same with the people you call your parents."

Tessa believed him.

A few seconds later, he was back with Phoebe. She was eighty pounds of wire and bone, as angry as a wet cat, but he carried her with ease, one hand over her mouth and the other wrapped around both her arms and her torso. After unlocking the door on the other side, he nudged it open with his knee. He tossed Phoebe onto the other seat and slammed the door.

Phoebe's eyes went wide at the sight of Tessa. "Tessa," she gasped. "Are you okay?" Her damp hands cupped Tessa's face, her tear-filled blue eyes only inches away.

"Do you still have your phone?" Tessa whispered urgently.

Phoebe's voice shook. "No."

Sinclair was already climbing back inside the SUV. He started it and drove off.

Phoebe slumped beside Tessa. She kept her eyes fastened on Tessa's face, as if trusting her to fix everything.

"Where are you taking us?" Tessa demanded.

"Manners."

"Can you please tell me where you're taking us?" When he still didn't speak, she forced herself to add "Dad."

Phoebe shot her a look but didn't say anything.

"To meet your mom, like I said. To meet Ruth."

Phoebe opened her mouth, but Tessa gave a short, sharp shake of her head. She had a feeling Sinclair would be more than willing to kill her sister if he thought she was too much trouble or even started to make a fuss. Instead of speaking, Phoebe pressed her wet face against Tessa's shoulder.

After a few turns, Tessa recognized the road they were on. It was the one they had taken to Gina's house. She pictured Victor driving, El in the back seat, the day they had thought would finally bring them answers.

But all it had brought was death.

The thought of her friends made Tessa want to crumple, but she couldn't. Right now, she had to focus on keeping herself and Phoebe alive. At a minimum, Phoebe. Phoebe, who had no connection to this man. Who was only caught up in these terrible circumstances because of Tessa. Phoebe, who was now curled against her, her slender shoulders shaking.

The street Sinclair turned onto was crowded with cars. Even inside the SUV, Tessa could hear loud rhythmic sounds. People chanting. Four syllables, repeated over and over. And then she picked out the words.

"Let's go, defense! Let's go, defense!"

They passed a sign for Brookwillow High School. It must be game night.

"My mother's here?" Tessa said, trying to understand. "At Brookwillow?"

"Yes."

He pulled over and parked in an empty handicapped space. "I'm going to have your sister undo your handcuffs, but don't try anything. I'll be holding a gun on her the whole time."

He showed the gun to Phoebe before getting out. After opening the door next to Tessa, he ordered Phoebe out of the car. She clambered over Tessa. Then he gave her the tiny handcuff key and explained how to undo Tessa's cuffs. Turning to face the interior, Tessa presented her wrists. Her sister's cool fingers trembled. Her breath on Tessa's nape was fast and jerky. Then he pocketed the handcuffs while telling Tessa to get out of the car.

As she did, Tessa frantically scanned the sidewalks for someone who might help her. They were empty. It seemed everyone who was going to the game was already there.

He marched them toward the stadium, with Tessa in the lead. They passed the cavernous area under the bleachers, then rounded the corner of the stands, past uniformed band members lined up and awaiting their cue. From the concession stand came the smell of popcorn and hot dogs. Tessa repressed the urge to vomit. The bleachers were packed, some fans clapping, others shouting encouragement. Parents clutched coffee cups or phones, keeping one eye on the game and another on younger siblings playing in the aisles.

Bright stadium lights illuminated players in blue and white chasing others in black and red. On the sideline, cheerleaders kicked and chanted, their pom-poms flashing silver.

Tessa kept turning to make sure Phoebe was right on her heels. She always was, but Sinclair's left arm was around her shoulders, his grip tight on her biceps. His right hand rested on the butt of his pistol, ready to draw it at any moment.

Tessa was still scanning the crowd looking for Ruth, even though another part of her knew it must be an impossibility. She turned back to Sinclair again.

"You said you were taking me to meet my mother."

"I am. She's right here. I think underneath section B." And then Sinclair pasted a smile on his face as he made his voice higher, a singsong.

"Your father was good to me." The words were the ones Tessa had watched and heard Ruth say. Sinclair switched back to his regular voice. "It's a wonder what you can do with AI."

Before she could fully grasp his meaning, the referee's whistle cut through the air. The players started running off the field as the cheerleaders finished their final cheer.

A man wearing a dark suit stepped out onto the green expanse. His bald head shone under the lights, as did the silver cordless microphone in his hand.

"Ladies and gentlemen, for the halftime show, I present to you the Brookwillow—" The emcee stopped before saying "marching band," confused by the three people moving toward him. His expression morphed to one of fear. Tessa looked over her shoulder. Quentin had pulled the gun from his holster and was now pointing it right at the emcee. When Quentin reached him, the emcee let the microphone be pulled from his slack hand. He raised his hands and started walking backward toward the relative safety of the crowd behind him, his eyes never leaving the gun.

KEISHA

Live to Tell

KEISHA WAS WALKING INTO HER APARTMENT WHEN her phone buzzed with a group text to all the task force. The Phantom had reportedly set a storage unit on fire in North Portland. The location was only a few miles away. Maybe she could get there first.

Back outside, Keisha slapped the portable siren on top of her car. Adrenaline turned her insides to liquid. It took three tries to fit the key into the ignition, but she finally managed and began speeding toward the storage complex. According to the two teens who had called 911, the unit had held the Phantom's trophies. But even more important—they claimed he had kidnapped Tessa Lundgren before locking them inside with the fire he had set.

Ignoring how her car bottomed out every time she hit a pothole, Keisha kept her foot pressed on the accelerator. Finally, she spotted three patrol cars and two fire engines next to a still smoldering storage unit.

After driving under the open gate, she skidded to a stop in front of two teens standing with a patrol officer. Both of their faces were smudged with smoke.

"I'm Keisha Washington," she said. "Tell me what happened. Where's Tessa?"

"Tessa told us about you," the guy said through a ragged cough. "The Phantom took her."

The girl said, "But I have that app called Where U At, the one that tracks your friends? I've been checking it. It looks like first they went to Bridgetown University, then Tessa's house. Now they're driving west."

"Give me your phone." Keisha held out her hand.

The girl stepped back so she was shoulder to shoulder with the guy. "If you're going to go find her, you have to take us with you."

You never put civilians in danger. Ever. But how much time would Keisha lose if she argued? "Get in the car," she said. Ignoring how the beat cop's mouth fell open, she pointed at the girl. "Sit by me and tell me where to go."

"I'm Victor and that's El," the guy said as he climbed into the back seat and Keisha started the car.

El's eyes were glued to her phone. "They just turned onto Highway 26."

What was out that way? And then Keisha knew. It was where Ruth McCoy grew up. That couldn't be a coincidence. She updated dispatch, then said to the teens, "Tell me more about what happened tonight."

"Tessa has been messaging with Ruth," Victor said.

Keisha let out an exasperated huff. "I doubt that very much." In front of her a minivan slowed to a crawl instead of pulling over. Teeth clenched, she whipped her car around.

El stuck up for her friend. "She even had a video call with her."

"AI's gotten good enough they can make you think you're talking to anyone," Keisha said. "A pop star, the president. A mom you've never met."

"Well, she, or whoever it was, said if Tessa came to this storage unit, they could meet. And Tessa wanted to meet her mom so bad. Of course we weren't going to let her go alone." El coughed and struggled to stop. "But when we got there, nobody was there. And the whole place was like a shrine to the Phantom, with scrapbooks and displays of things he'd taken from victims."

Victor leaned forward. "The unit smelled like oil or something, but by the time we realized it was also starting to smell like smoke, it was too late. This guy burst in, grabbed Tessa, dragged her out, and locked us in. She was trying to fight him, but he was too strong."

"What did he look like?" Keisha asked. They were the first two people to see the Phantom and live to tell about it. She just hoped Tessa would be the third.

"Just some middle-aged white guy with a shaved head, all dressed in black." Victor exhaled sharply. "I was more focused on Tessa. After he dragged her out, I heard her scream, but then it was cut off. I think he hit her."

Keisha's eyes flicked to Victor's face in her rearview mirror. He looked miserable.

"Then what happened?" She was nearly to Highway 26.

"We tried to call 911, but neither of our phones worked. Then El noticed the walls didn't go all the way to the top. The last bit's chicken wire, probably for airflow. But the air was still getting smoky, real fast."

El used two fingers to zoom in on the map. "It looks like they just took exit seventy-three."

Keisha again relayed the information to dispatch. Because everyone had been heading to the storage complex, she was still the closest unit to the Phantom. "We're about six miles behind them," she said.

"Can't we go any faster?" Victor asked.

Keisha shook her head. "I'm already doing eighty. Even at this speed, I probably won't have time to react if someone does something stupid." All it took was one distracted driver. "But if he's keeping to the speed limit, I should make that up soon."

"The speed limit here is fifty," Victor said, "so it will take about twelve minutes for us to catch up."

Keisha couldn't do math in her head like that,

but it sounded right. It also sounded too long. She risked goosing it up to eighty-five, praying no one would suddenly pull in front of them. "How did you two get out?" she asked.

"I found some scissors in a desk drawer," Victor said. "We pushed the desk against the wall, got on top, and I boosted up El so she could cut the wire. Only it was too thick. And then I lost my balance and we both fell off. I was so frustrated I kicked the wall. It made a hole, so we both started kicking."

"Then I remembered the scissors and started stabbing." El mimed the motion.

"We were finally able to squeeze between the two by fours," Victor said. "The only problem was the next door was locked, too, and the smoke was spreading."

El peered at her phone. "It looks like they just turned onto Foothills Road."

Keisha relayed the new information to dispatch as she tried to mentally map the area. Was he taking her to the McCoys?

Victor cleared his ragged throat. "So we just kept repeating the process until we found an empty unit with an unlocked door. Once we were out, we had to run a couple of blocks before our cell phones worked. And we called 911."

El spoke over his last few words, her tone urgent. "It looks like they're at Brookwillow High School."

"That's where Ruth McCoy went to school." Keisha updated dispatch. They were less than a mile away, but increasing traffic had forced her to slow down.

El enlarged the map. "They might be at the football stadium? Wherever they are, I think they've stopped."

"Good," Keisha said. But was it? Because while Tessa had probably been safe when he was driving, now the Phantom must be taking the next step in his plan.

And she had no doubt there was a plan.

They were just pulling up to the stadium when they heard the boom and echo of a gunshot, followed by screaming.

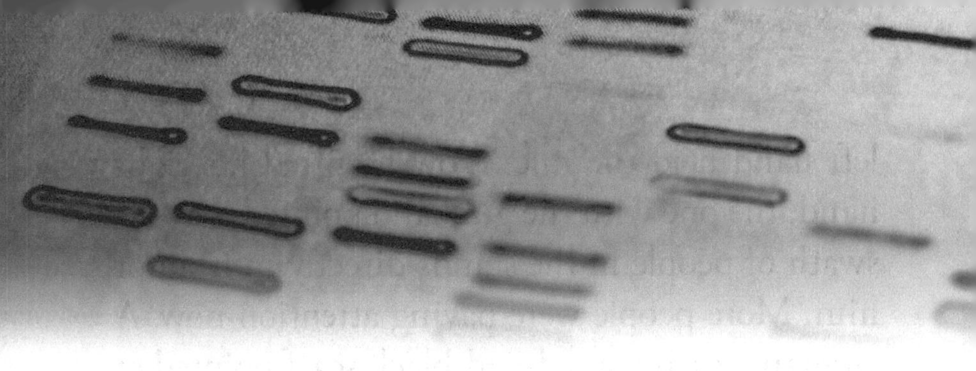

TESSA

Boneless

SINCLAIR HAD A GUN AND PHOEBE. HE ALSO HAD the mic.

Tessa had nothing.

After a whine of feedback, Sinclair said, "Ladies and gentlemen, I'd like to introduce myself. I'm the man you've all feared for years: the Portland Phantom."

A few people gasped, but most of the crowd in the bleachers seemed more confused than frightened. Many were still checking their phones or chatting with their neighbors.

Quentin's left arm was looped around Phoebe's shoulders, pressing her against him, and his left hand held the mic. Now he lifted his right hand, the one with the gun, and pointed it at the swath of people in the stands directly in front of him. More people were paying attention now. A woman wearing a red-and-black scarf pointed at Sinclair and screamed.

"May I introduce my daughter, Tessa." He half turned toward her, while still speaking into the mic. "Tessa, I'd like you to take this gun and start killing people. If you don't, I'll strangle Phoebe. Your so-called sister."

People began to scramble out of the stands directly in front of him, or at least they tried to. It quickly turned to chaos: pushing, shoving, tripping. A large man pushed a white-haired woman out of the way. She fell and did not get up.

Sinclair handed Tessa the gun, which was surprisingly heavy. Rather than pointing it at the crowd, she let it dangle at her side. She focused on his left hand, now encircling Phoebe's neck. She was so small his hand went most of the way around her sister's throat. With one squeeze, Sinclair could stop the air from going into Phoebe's lungs, keep the blood from her brain.

He held her tight against his torso, protecting

all his own vital organs. He crouched so his head was next to Phoebe's. He was grinning at Tessa. The grin of a man who was determined to make them all dance to his tune.

This was it, Tessa realized. His ultimate act of power would be this public, shocking display. It would ensure his name was immortalized. While more and more people were managing to exit the stands, at least a dozen camera phones were now trained on him. Even the local TV station, here to film the big game, had switched their camera to focus on him.

Sinclair was playing with all of them: Tessa, her family, law enforcement, the media, even social media. He was the puppet master, the center of attention.

Not knowing what else to do, Tessa raised the gun and pointed it at the crowd. More people screamed or dove to the ground or pushed toward the exits. A dark-haired woman was yelling frantically, "Cameron! Where are you? Cameron!"

Could Tessa possibly shoot Phoebe in some place a bullet would pass through her slight body without doing too much damage—but still kill Sinclair? No. The risk was too high. The same with trying to shoot him in the head, which was so close to Phoebe's.

"Tessa," he warned, his fingers flexing on her sister's throat. "You have ten seconds."

What could she do? No matter what she chose, Sinclair would win. If she didn't start shooting people, he would strangle Phoebe. And he'd make sure she watched him do it. If she shot people, he would still probably kill Phoebe, and then strangers would be dead by Tessa's hand. Any choice she made would be one he wanted her to make.

In his mind, Tessa was simply a woman. And a woman could never be a threat.

Could she use that arrogance to her advantage?

Sinclair was bigger. Stronger. Completely willing to hurt Phoebe, Tessa, or anyone else, without a second's hesitation.

Tessa could not fight her biological father on his terms. He would always win.

"It's time, Tessa," he said.

Phoebe screamed, or started to. Immediately, the sound was choked off.

Adrenaline flaring like lightning in her veins, Tessa desperately pointed at the sky and pulled the trigger. The gun kicked in her hands and the panic in the crowd ratcheted up even higher. A man in a yellow shirt standing near the top of the stands either jumped or fell twenty feet to the ground and started screaming. People were frantically trying to get away, but the stands were too crowded. Some of the more athletic were vaulting over seats. An older man was simply frozen, eyes squeezed shut. As if he didn't see the bad thing, then it couldn't hurt him.

"Not good enough, Tessa," Sinclair said into the microphone. "Start killing people or I kill your sister."

So what were her strengths? What could Tessa do that Sinclair couldn't?

"Kill them or I kill her."

Love.

Tessa turned back to him, this man who had tried to claim he was her father. Sinclair ducked, shielding more of himself behind Phoebe. As he did, his arm loosened a bit.

"Boneless, Phoebe!" Tessa shouted. "Boneless!"

Phoebe sagged, dead weight, and Sinclair lost his grip on her.

And in that instant, Tessa pulled the trigger.

**Update to the Lifetime documentary
*Chasing Shadows: The Hunt for the Portland
Phantom***

The camera opens with a close-up of Maxwell Holloway. In the two years since the documentary's initial broadcast, his craggy face has acquired even more pleats.

"Welcome to the latest update of *Chasing Shadows.* Thanks to some amazing teenagers, we now know the identity of the Portland Phantom. And one of the people who uncovered the Phantom's true identity was actually his biological daughter."

The camera pulls back to reveal a young woman sitting next to Holloway.

Tessa Lundgren.

He leans forward. "Tessa, can I ask what it's been like, learning who your father was?"

She shrugs. "That's the thing. He's not really my father. Quentin Sinclair is just the man who seduced my mother, Ruth McCoy, when she was only a high school freshman and Sinclair was her school resource officer. But my real parents, my true parents, are the ones who raised me. Lars and Lena Lundgren."

"And how did the Phantom use Ruth, your biological mother, against you?" Holloway manages to look as if he doesn't already know the answer.

"Sinclair used AI to pretend to be my mom, including on a video call. All to lure me to him. Eventually, he admitted she was buried under the football stadium at her old high school. The police later located her remains."

"And you discovered the Phantom had actually killed your mother the same day you were born, is that right?"

"Sinclair had leukemia when he was a child and had to have a bone marrow transplant. Ninety-nine point nine percent of the time, the treatment causes sterility. So when Ruth came to school and told him about giving birth to me, he was sure she'd cheated on him. After he strangled her, he buried her body on the stadium's construction site."

Holloway leans forward. "And that bone marrow transplant is also what led to the wrong man being detained for the Phantom's crimes."

Tessa nods. "Your bone marrow creates your blood. So after a bone marrow transplant, your blood becomes identical to your donor's. When Sinclair murdered Wren Phillips and placed an item from the previous victim, Alida Cleary, on her body, he also accidentally left behind a drop of blood. When the police tested that blood, it was a match to Frank Porter, the man who donated his bone marrow to Sinclair decades ago."

"And Porter has since been released from jail," Holloway interjects.

"That's right. He had nothing to do with it."

Even more wrinkles appear on Holloway's brow. "It must be painful, knowing you can never actually meet your mother."

"Biological mother," Tessa corrects. "I still have my mother who raised me. And now I'm getting to know Ruth's brother. My uncle. We talk all the time. So I have more people who love me in my life, not fewer."

"Are you in any kind of touch with your biological father? With Quentin Sinclair? I know he's being held in the Multnomah County jail."

Tessa makes a face as if she has tasted something bad. "No." After the silence stretches out, she elaborates. "I guess I'll have to see him at the trial. But it was clear I didn't matter to him, except as some kind of reflection. He wanted to ensure I was truly his by making me follow in his footsteps. He was trying to goad me into killing someone.

The people at the football game, or even him. If I had actually killed him, I think he would have been happy."

"Instead, you shot him in the right shoulder."

Tessa bites her lip and looks away. "I'd like to say I shot him there on purpose, but I'd never fired a gun before that night. I'm just lucky I didn't kill him. Killing someone, even someone as evil as him, would have to damage a person." She sighs. "I still have nightmares about what happened. And when I do, my parents wake me up. But the man who wanted to claim me as his child never comforted me after a nightmare. He didn't teach me to ride a bike. He didn't take care of me when I was sick. He didn't encourage me to write stories. My real parents, the ones who adopted me, they did that."

TESSA

Sweet

ON THE LAST DAY BEFORE CHRISTMAS BREAK, MOST of the teachers let students watch movies. But Mr. Prenty was not one to follow the crowd. When Tessa walked into biology, "Protein Synthesis Lab" was written on the board. Next to Mr. Prenty was a covered rolling cart that must have held the chemicals they'd need.

"What's the latest on your dad?" Victor asked as Tessa slid into the seat next to him.

"He's definitely getting better." When her dad had learned his scans were negative, his anxiety had dramatically decreased, and that had helped both his appetite and mood. The doctors' best guess was that he had picked up an infection doing the obstacle course race. "Last night he ate almost his whole dinner."

"That's great news." Victor reached into his backpack and produced a small black box tied with a ribbon. "In case I don't see you before Christmas, I wanted to give this to you."

"You shouldn't have." But she was already pulling the silver ribbon.

Inside, a pen lay nestled in white tissue paper. When Tessa picked it up, it was surprisingly heavy, silver with a royal-blue barrel. The engraving caught the light. She tilted the pen to read the words.

For signing the first of many.

Tears sprang to her eyes. "Oh, Victor!"

"At your first book signing, I expect you to use it." He pushed back his dark sweep of hair.

"Of course!"

After everything, Tessa had become the center of a media frenzy, both social and old school, ranging from TikToks to *60 Minutes.* One woman reached out multiple times. She wrote true crime, but her books were well-reviewed, lauded for their literary flair.

Should Tessa talk to her? Initially, her parents

discouraged the idea. But she had discussed the pros and cons with them, as well as with the counselor she now saw once a week. And when she and her parents read some of the author's previous books, they found they focused on the victims, not the perpetrators.

No matter what Tessa did, there would be books about her and her biological father. With her parents' blessing, she had agreed to cooperate with the author—on the condition she could also collaborate. The author had moved into a nearby Airbnb, and Tessa now joined her after school, writing the first drafts of any scene that involved her, using her coauthor's feedback to make them better. It was both exhausting and energizing. The book, titled *Not My Father's Daughter*, would publish with both their bylines in June, the same week Tessa graduated.

Tessa returned the pen to its box. "I never would have figured everything out if it weren't for you and El."

Victor bit his lip, distracting her for a second. His teeth were very white and his lips very red. She was beginning to think he saw her only as a friend. "I'm sorry the answers weren't what you wanted."

"But they were the truth. And that's what I needed."

At the front of the class, Mr. Prenty clapped his hands as soon as the bell rang. "Today we're going to be learning about transcription and translation. These processes work together to make proteins using the instructions written in the DNA code. In today's lab, you will be mimicking protein synthesis by decoding a strand of DNA using a codon table."

As students sighed or propped tired heads on fists, Mr. Prenty whipped the white plastic tablecloth off the rolling cart. Instead of holding beakers and chemicals, there were boxes of sugar cookies, tubes of colored icing, and plastic bowls of toppings: mini chocolate chips, green and red M&Ms, coconut shreds, colored sprinkles, and more. Frowns turned into smiles.

"First you'll go out in the hallway, which is now the nucleus, to receive a cookie gene recipe. While you're there, you'll model transcription by converting DNA into MRNA. Then you'll return to this classroom—which is now the ribosome—to model translation."

As Mr. Prenty spoke, under the table Victor's

cool hand slid into hers. He squeezed, softly at first, and then a little harder. Tessa was suddenly aware of every centimeter of skin, both hers and his. All her muscles were humming, even the tiny ones in her toes.

"Wait a minute," Trey said. "Are you saying we're going to be decorating cookies in biology class?"

"That's not what I have written on my planner," Mr. Prenty said with a rare smile. "It says we will use a codon table to translate a genetic code into a sequence of amino acids. The fact those amino acids are represented by cookie toppings is immaterial."

"Sweet," Trey said.

"Yes it is," Victor agreed, looking right at Tessa.

A NOTE FROM THE AUTHOR

After both my parents died, I ended up with a lot of hundred-year-old family photos, most of them unlabeled. Neither of my parents had known much about their family history past the names of their grandparents. After they were gone, my brother, sister, and I all took DNA tests, and then I spent years building a family tree. Sometimes that tree had unexpected branches, like second cousins whose on-paper fathers were not their biological fathers. The further back in my family's past I went, the more tangled it got. One great-grandfather was a murderer, another an arsonist. My third great-grandfather seems to have faked his own death and then remarried (twice!). My ninth great-grandfather narrowly escaped hanging after he was accused of bewitching a pig in 1656.

This book allowed me to explore biology, destiny, and self-determination. And it let me talk to some fascinating people. Any errors are my own.

Nathan Adams, a systems engineer at Forensic Bioinformatics, helped me understand how and why my killer might leave a drop of blood behind, and how it would be discovered.

Caron Pruiett, a specialist in using scientific methods to identify humans, talked to me about bone marrow transplants, DNA, and law enforcement.

I found Leah Larkin, PhD, genetic genealogist, through her fascinating blog, theDNAgeek.com. She helped me think about percentages and scenarios to make my fictional story fit reality.

Patty Drabing, director and president of dnaadoption.com, which many adoptees have used to find their birth families, helped me understand more about GEDmatch and investigative genetic genealogy matching.

Ron Turker, MD, orthopedic surgeon and an author in his own right, has become my go-to doctor for any and all book-related medical questions. If he is not certain about an answer, he has a whole network of physician friends he can ask.

Lee Etten, fire captain/paramedic at Portland Fire & Rescue's Training Division, helped me with my fictional fire.

In the course of my research, I discovered a private message board for self-storage owners, and they graciously allowed me to pose some questions. A user named Hilltop_Bob (real name Kevin Heide) was especially helpful in thinking up ways my characters could escape if they were trapped in a burning storage unit.

Robin Burcell, former cop and now an award-winning author, is always game to answer my questions about police procedure, evidence, and more.

In the Blood is my seventeenth book with my editor and publisher Christy Ottaviano and my thirty-first book with my agent Wendy Schmalz. With every book, they push me to new heights.

In addition to Christy and Wendy, it took a team of dedicated and talented people to put this book in your hands, including the production team: Jake Regier, Tracy Koontz, Erin

Slonaker, Kimberly Stella, and Erica Huang; the design team: Karina Granda, Gabrielle Chang, and jacket artist Neil Swaab; and the marketing and publicity teams: Victoria Stapleton, Christie Michel, Bill Grace, Emilie Polster, Kelly Moran, and Savannah Kennelly. Additional thanks go to Olivia McKeon, Jackie Engel, and Megan Tingley.

My booking agent, Carmen Oliver at TheBookingBiz.com, is worth her weight in books. With her assistance, I am able to speak to thousands of students each year.

APRIL HENRY

is a *New York Times* bestselling author of many acclaimed mysteries for adults and over fifteen novels for teens, including *Girl, Stolen*; *Girl Forgotten*, which won the Edgar Award for Best Young Adult Mystery; *Two Truths and a Lie*, which was a YALSA Quick Pick for Reluctant Young Adult Readers; and *The Girl I Used to Be*, which was an Edgar Award finalist and won the Anthony Award for Best YA Novel. She lives in Oregon and invites you to visit her at aprilhenry.com.

FROM *NEW YORK TIMES* BESTSELLING AUTHOR

APRIL HENRY

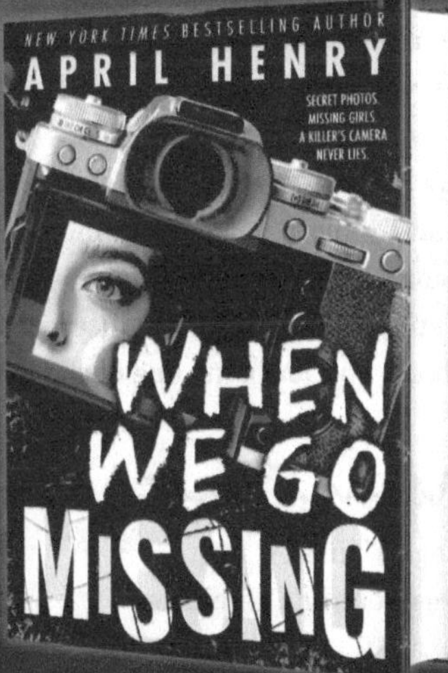

Christy Ottaviano Books

NOVL

theNOVL.com

CELEBRATING 100 YEARS OF PUBLISHING

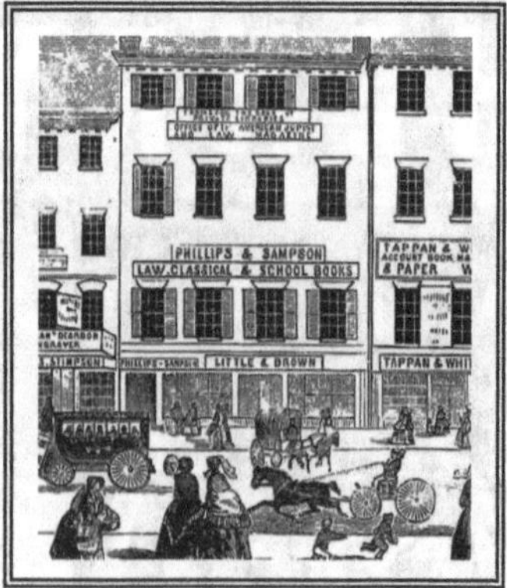

Dear Reader,

You may have noticed the words "Little, Brown and Company" on the title page of this book and wondered what they mean. Well, Charles C. Little and James Brown were the founders of this publishing house, and the "and Company" is all the editors, designers, marketers, publicists, salespeople, and more who help produce each book and bring it to readers like you. Little, Brown was founded in Boston, Massachusetts, in 1837, and some of its early publications included *The Writings of George Washington* and *The Works of Benjamin Franklin*. The catalog grew to feature works by Emily Dickinson and Louisa May Alcott, among many other notable authors. In 1926, recognizing that the literature we read when we are young has a deep and lasting influence and requires expert curation, the company appointed an editor to lead a dedicated children's department.

In 2026, Little, Brown Books for Young Readers celebrates one hundred years of excellence in publishing. Today, we are a division of Hachette Livre, the third-largest publisher in the world, and we are based in New York City. Our staff has grown from a team of two to more than one hundred people. And with the changes in technology, our books are read by more readers, in more ways, and in more countries than ever before. However, one thing has not changed: our commitment to providing a supportive home for all creators and superb stories for all readers. Thank you for being one of them.

Megan Tingley
President and Publisher

To learn more about Little, Brown's history, authors, and books, please visit LBYR.com.